For Vic S.-C., who likes to weave words too...

Scholastic Children's Books
An imprint of Scholastic Ltd
Euston House, 24 Eversholt Street, London, NW1 1DB, UK
Registered office: Westfield Road, Southam, Warwickshire, CV47 0RA
SCHOLASTIC and associated logos are trademarks and/or
registered trademarks of Scholastic Inc.

First published in the UK by Scholastic Ltd, 2016

Text copyright © Karen McCombie, 2016

The right of Karen McCombie to be identified
as the author of this work has been asserted by her.

ISBN 978 1407 16409 0

A CIP catalogue record for this book
is available from the British Library.

Printed by CPI Group (UK) Ltd, Croydon, CR0 4YY
Papers used by Scholastic Children's Books are made
from wood grown in sustainable forests.

1 3 5 7 9 10 8 6 4 2

www.scholastic.co.uk

When your world isn't turning,
And your path leads nowhere,
Don't be scared, keep on walking,
Turn the corner, I'll be there...

From "Turn the Corner", by White Star Line

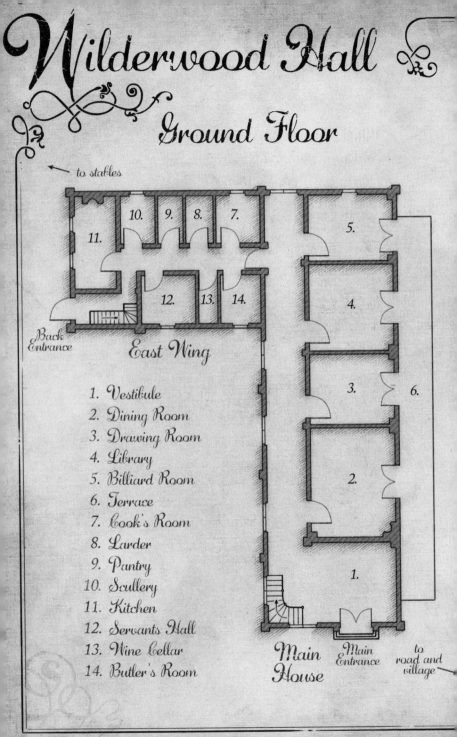

Wilderwood Hall

Ground Floor

to stables

10.   9.   8.   7.

11.

5.

12.   13.   14.

4.

Back
Entrance

East Wing

3.   6.

1. Vestibule
2. Dining Room
3. Drawing Room
4. Library
5. Billiard Room
6. Terrace
7. Cook's Room
8. Larder
9. Pantry
10. Scullery
11. Kitchen
12. Servants Hall
13. Wine Cellar
14. Butler's Room

2.

1.

*Main
House*

Main
Entrance

to
road and
village

First Floor

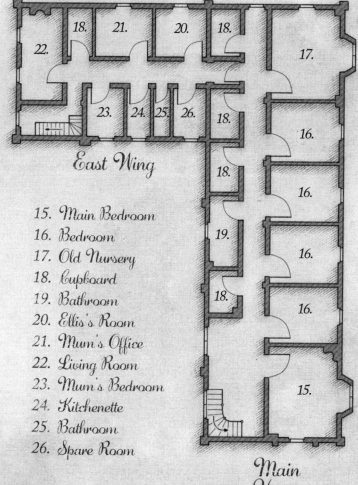

East Wing

15. Main Bedroom
16. Bedroom
17. Old Nursery
18. Cupboard
19. Bathroom
20. Ellis's Room
21. Mum's Office
22. Living Room
23. Mum's Bedroom
24. Kitchenette
25. Bathroom
26. Spare Room

Main House

The world is whirling, tilting, shifting. And I have nothing to hold on to – except for a posy of eye-meltingly pink gerberas.

So I close my eyes and try to wish the bad feeling away.

"Congratulations!" I hear the registrar say brightly. "You may now kiss the bride!"

OK, so maybe I'd better *not* keep my eyes closed. It wouldn't look too good, my mother being legally married for all of three seconds and me blanking it out. So I bite my lip, and force my eyes wide open.

(Whirl, tilt, shift. . .)

All around me, cheers break out, as Mum and RJ

throw their arms around each other and smooch madly.

All *I* can do is try not to be sick.

"Woo-hoo!" hollers someone behind me, at a pitch that nearly punctures my eardrums.

I don't turn around, but guess it's probably the drummer in RJ's band. He also does backing vocals, and his voice is so loud he practically doesn't need a microphone, Mum says. She's seen the band play live, so she should know.

Oh, I think I really *might* be sick. As the early spring breeze buffets my loose long hair, I take a few deep breaths and hope that'll help. It doesn't much.

"Sadie looks beautiful, doesn't she?" says Dolores, suddenly nudging me with her elbow. Dolores's fabulous halo of an Afro frames her face, and her eyes are masked by giant, expensive sunglasses – but I can still see the sentimental tears streaking her soft brown cheeks.

"Yes," I manage to mumble.

Well, duh, Mum *always* looks beautiful. No one's going to argue with that. But I guess today she's looking *extra* beautiful in her bride-white, especially since Mum's version of bride-white is a vintage

2

1960s short lace dress, with waxy camellias pinned into her messy, pink-tipped blonde hair.

She's also wearing flat strappy sandals, and has to stand on her tiptoes to lip-sync with RJ, even though he's bending down and tenderly pulling Mum up towards his towering, ultra-skinny self.

"Can you believe this?" says Dolores, snuffling into a tissue she's pulled from her red leather handbag. "Three months ago, Sadie and RJ didn't even know each other existed!"

"Well, technically, Mum *did* already know RJ," I correct her, as I try to keep myself together by squeezing my neon-pink nails into my palms. Of course Mum knew RJ. Or at least knew *of* RJ Johnstone and his band, White Star Line. Plenty of people do. I mean, personally, I've never been into White Star Line's music, but they're the sort of old, 1990s indie rock band that gets called "legendary" a lot. The sort that still tour constantly and play sets at festivals where devoted fans bellow along to every last lyric and forgive them for their hair going grey around the edges. And even old Mr Evans in the flat opposite ours knows one of White Star Line's tracks; it's the very bass-y sounding one that got used over the opening credits of that detective series on BBC One recently.

"Ah, yes, of course! Silly me." Dolores laughs at herself as she dabs the tears away. "You know, I've cried so much today I think my brain's gone soggy."

Dolores is Mum's agent. *And* her friend, when she's not busy booking Mum work as a hair and make-up artist. So I guess she's partly crying 'cause that's what people do at their friends' weddings, and partly crying 'cause she's about to lose one of her most reliable and popular stylists.

The other hair and make-up artists at Dolores's agency can be a bit snobby and insist they'll *only* work with gorgeous models for glamorous magazine shoots or snooty catwalk shows. Mum's not like that. I mean, until half a minute ago, she was a single mother, bringing me up on her own. Which meant she was always more than happy to do *any* job, even if it was just powdering the sweaty forehead of a random actor in an ad for a verruca treatment, or an online bingo site, or for a toilet cleaner or something.

And then – exactly eleven and a half weeks ago – Dolores took a booking for Mum that would change everything. *Everything.* Yep, Dolores didn't realize she was playing the accidental cupid when she sent Mum off to the video shoot for "Turn the Corner", White Star Line's latest single...

"Ellis? Ellis, baby?" I hear Mum call out.

Everyone around me – and that's a crowd which includes famous faces from bands and a couple of DJs I recognize too – starts oohing and ahhing and stares from me to my beautiful mum and back again.

Even on a normal day, that would make the anxiety waves roll right in; I love my mum, but I don't love people comparing us. We're not exactly similar. My best friend, Shaniya, once said it was as if this tiny punk fairy had given birth to a giraffe. *Thanks*, Shaniya. But she's got a point. I'm all gangly long arms and legs, and even though I'm only thirteen, I'm still a head taller than Mum. (Tall and shy is a pretty tough combination.)

And today . . . well, it's not exactly a normal day. So right this second, I'm facing a *tsunami* of anxiety, with all these strangers around me, and Mum's in so such a love bubble she's not really there for me in the way she usually is.

On top of that, here I am, struggling not to barf.

"Come here, baby girl!" Mum says, holding out both her hands to me.

RJ has an arm around her tiny waist, and looks as ecstatic as someone who's just won the lottery.

Though he'll never need that kind of money; RJ's got so much spare cash that he can do stuff like go and buy a mansion in the wilds of Scotland on a complete whim. . .

"Ellis? C'mere, please!" Mum smiles at me, her lips the colour of glossy pink icing on Krispy Kreme doughnuts.

I try to smile back, I really do. Taking a shaky step towards Mum, I clutch the stems of my gerbera posy so tightly I feel the soft stems snap and—

Nope, I can't do this. I have to get out of here NOW.

"Ellis? Ellis! Wait!" Mum calls after me as I push through the throng and get as far away from her and her new husband as possible. . .

Slap, *slap*.
  Slap, *slap*.
  Slap, *slap*.

I concentrate on the rhythm of the grey-brown water gently lapping the hull of the boat and feel my heart rate finally slow. It's funny, but the hollowness of the sound almost matches the song that's now playing in the background.

What is it again?

I can't quite make it out 'cause of the clamour of chat and laughter from the celebrating crowd up on the bow. It's some old '60s soul thing, I know *that* much, since Mum and RJ bonded over their mutual love of Motown and wanted that to be the soundtrack of their wedding. Their identical taste in music is one of the million coincidences that made them totally – and ultra-quickly – convinced they were meant to be together.

"Hey, are you riding the waves again, baby?" Mum asks, assuming anxiety's got me on the run. "Remember it rolls right in, Ellis, but it always rolls back out again."

As she reassures me, her hand begins to swirl comforting circles between my shoulder blades.

Oh, that feels good, I think as I lean on the handrail, my eyes still fixed on the choppy Thames below.

"Actually, it's not that," I tell her. "I knew I was going to be sick, and I didn't want to spoil your moment by vomiting on your guests."

"Oh, Ellis! That's *my* fault," says Mum, and immediately her hand lifts from my back. Click goes the sound of a clasp, and the next thing I hear is frantic rummaging.

"I've been *so* busy organizing everything for today I didn't even *think* about the fact that you should've taken a travel-sickness pill! Here, have one now and it should kick in soon."

I warily straighten up and turn to her. She might be a bride, but Mum's still a one-woman organizational wizard. From her mini patent handbag she's pulled a small packet of pills and another of wet wipes.

"Hey, *I* forgot too," I say, and let Mum place the sugary tablet on my tongue and clean me up, as if I were still her little girl.

"Well, this *is* a pretty amazing wedding venue," Mum says with a smile, "it's just a bit on the wobbly side, eh?"

"Uh-huh," I agree with her as she uses another wipe on my forehead and neck to cool me down.

If I didn't feel ill, I could properly appreciate being on this boat, cruising past famous sights like the Houses of Parliament and the London Eye. (Apparently, it's something *else* that can happen when you're a successful and well-off musician; you ask your personal assistant to scour Last-Minute-But-Amazing-Venues-For-Your-Wedding.com, and magically, it's done.)

The thing is, maybe it's not only the boat that's made me feel travel-sick. Maybe it's the speed everything's happened lately. Like. . .

Surprise! Mum has fallen in love in about two seconds flat.

Surprise! Mum's new boyfriend has asked her to marry him on their first date.

Surprise! It wasn't just a joke, and Mum gives in and answers "yes" on their *sixth* date.

Surprise! RJ says, "Why wait? Why not get married straight away?" Mum says, "Why not?"

The speed of the wedding in particular caught loads of people out. Granny and Uncle Ben and my cousins couldn't make it from Australia in time, even though RJ offered to pay for their flights. And RJ's eighteen-year-old daughter didn't come either, and she lives not *so* far away, in Somerset, with her mum. Though most of the time she's at boarding school, in Devon or somewhere – I forget.

But the surprises connected with Mum and RJ's love-a-thon don't stop with the wedding. There's one more game-changing surprise. Home isn't going to be a cosy flat for two in North London any more. It's going to be a dilapidated mansion for three, six hundred miles away.

A dilapidated mansion that's going to be Mum and RJ's Shiny New Project.

Well, it's great that they've got this exciting venture to look forward to. But excuse me if I'm not so excited. Excuse me if I feel pretty miserable, giving up my life and my friends here in London.

"Wow, this time next week we'll be saying goodbye to all of this," says Mum, as if she's only just noticed the spectacular view of world-famous tourist landmarks. "Can you believe it, Ellis?"

I don't reply. Instead I picture all those images I saw on the property website. Wilderwood Hall in all its glory – joke! It's just this huge, brooding, grey granite building, with a warren of semi-derelict rooms inside and some tumbledown stables nearby, surrounded by a forest of tall, dense firs cutting it off from the world.

Then I picture something completely different: my busy, bustling school playground. Shaniya and the other girls, sitting on "our" bench at break time, giggling and laughing without me...

"Oh, baby, you're shivering!" Mum says, pulling me to her for a hug.

It's no surprise I'm shivering; getting married on the open deck of a boat in March is perhaps a bit optimistic.

"Hey, *Mrs Johnstone*, and the lovely Miss Harper! How's my little family?" I hear RJ ask.

Mum unwraps one arm from me and gives him a welcoming wave.

"We're good. Well, Ellis has a bit of motion sickness," Mum tells him.

"Oh, poor you," says RJ, frowning sympathetically at me. "My daughter's like that too. She and her mum joined us on tour in the US when she was little. She barfed her way across most of the west coast of America, I think!"

I look up at his smiling, friendly face and his floppy mess of a quiff – and I feel my tummy flip again. *This* time I don't think it is anything to do with the boat bobbing.

The thing is, from what I've seen of RJ, he's really, really nice and easy-going, but I don't feel ready for an all-of-a-sudden stepdad. It's just been me and Mum, always and for ever. And Shaniya might think I'm mad for not being ecstatic about Mum dating someone like RJ, but seeing Mum share part of her life with a person who isn't *me* is incredibly hard to get my head around.

Speaking of Shaniya (cue another tummy flip), she's going to go *completely* crazy when she finds out about the wedding. She's not going to understand why I wasn't allowed to tell her, never mind invite her. She'll be *deeply* offended that Mum worried Shaniya might gossip to someone, who'd tell someone, who'd tell someone who'd stick it on Facebook, and then Mum's secret wedding to RJ would be about as secret as the name of the prime minister.

So maybe the stress of that is getting to me too. Still, whatever the reasons, I mustn't, *mustn't* be sick in front of Mum and RJ. They'd probably see it as a bad omen for their marriage, their future togeth—

"Oi! NO! NO *WAY!!*" a shout shatters the moment, followed by more shouts and a whole lot of swearing.

"What's happening?" I ask nervously, staring at the cluster of wedding guests gathering at the railing around the right side of the boat.

"God ... it's the paparazzi," sighs RJ, slapping his forehead with his hand. "How did they find out about the wedding?"

At least I know it wasn't Shaniya, I think as my heart thunders at the sight of the speedboat growling alongside us. A comically huge lens is being aimed up at us, and the man behind it – his face hidden by both baseball cap and camera – click, click, clicks frantically.

Suddenly, it's all too much. *Everything* about today is too much. I'm dizzy and deafened and I grab hold of the railing.

"It'll pass, it'll pass, it'll pass," I frantically mutter to myself, leaning over to fix my eyes on the sludge-brown waves of the Thames, hoping they'll calm me again.

But straight away, I see something.

It's a face. . .

A face in the water, a girl's face, dark eyes staring back up at me through the murk.

(Whirl, tilt, shift.)

No, no, *no*! I'm not letting anxiety trick me and mess with my mind. There's *no one* in the water. It's just my own reflection, distorted by the churning river.

Feeling panicked and slightly mad, I squeeze my eyes tight closed, let go of the railing and press my palms hard over my ears. It's probably next to useless, but it's the best I can do to block out everything: the angry yelling, the head-drilling roar of the speedboat, the weird hall-of-mirrors version of me in the water and this whole crazy, alien version of life I seem to have suddenly found myself in.

If I could I'd turn and run.

But I have nowhere, absolutely nowhere, to run to. . .

Thunk.

That's the sound of my heart sinking, which is quite something, since I didn't think it could sink any further than it already has lately.

It's four o'clock on a Friday afternoon, and if life had carried on the way it was supposed to, today I'd be finished with school for the Easter holidays. I'd be playing around on my iPad on my bed, planning lazy trips to the local Odeon or maybe cool Camden Market with Shaniya.

But today is Day One of our *new-look* life. And after driving for hours and endless hours, me and Mum still haven't arrived at Wilderwood Hall. Instead, we seem to have accidentally found ourselves in a tartan museum.

"Can't we go somewhere else?" I whisper urgently as we both hesitate in the doorway of the Cairn Café.

"Ellis, there *is* nowhere else to go," Mum whispers back. "This is the only café in the only village for miles around. Anyway, maybe it'll have wifi."

I seriously doubt that.

Mum wants wifi to help us find our way to Wilderwood Hall, which can't be far, so that we'll be there in plenty of time to welcome the removal lorry. *I* want it because I'm desperate to find out what Shaniya's posted. She sent me a text saying *LOL LOL LOL – Instagram NOW!* before my signal died twenty miles ago. Hearing from her at all made my heart lurch; she hasn't spoken to me, not even to say goodbye, since she found out about the wedding.

Still, I reckon there's more chance of coming across the Loch Ness Monster in the Cairn Café's bathroom sink than an actual internet connection. I mean, look at the polyester tartan curtains, the plastic tartan tablecloths and the dusty dried thistle arrangements on every spare shelf and windowsill.

And what about that ancient TV balanced on the equally ancient video recorder? On the screen – in strangely lurid colours – a grinning, hairy man in a kilt is playing an accordion really, really badly.

This place is SO not going to have wifi.

What it *does* have is a white-haired waitress who looks like she should have retired decades ago.

There is just one customer – a bored-looking teenage boy with messy, fair hair practically down to his shoulders. Or maybe I should say there are *three* customers ... two black-and-white sheepdogs are by the boy's side. While he drinks from a can of Coke, they noisily slurp from a bowl of water on the cracked lino floor.

And get this: all of them – dogs included – are staring at me and Mum as if we've just beamed in from the planet Zorg. OK, I get it. This is the sort of village where everyone's families can be traced back to the Dark Ages – dogs included – at the very earliest, isn't it? Where they consider you "new" even if your great-grandmother was born here. Me and Mum, fresh from London this morning, don't stand a chance of fitting in. We should have got ourselves those badges the people at Pixar make their visitors wear: *Stranger, From the Outside*...

I slouch on to the nearest chair and try to will myself invisible, while Mum drops a plastic folder on to the table and shrugs off her parka, hanging it on the back of the chair beside me. My eye catches the pretty white star she's had tattooed on the inside of her left wrist. It matches one that RJ got years ago on the inside of his right wrist.

"Hello!" Mum calls across brightly to the elderly woman behind the counter. "Could we have –"

I'm aware of Mum's pause; she was about to ask for her usual Earl Grey, I'm sure, but has just spotted a box of bog-standard teabags and a jar of instant coffee parked beside a kettle. Asking for Earl Grey in this place would probably be like asking for ocelot on toast.

"– a pot of tea and an orange juice, please?" Mum asks with a friendly smile. "And could I just use your loo?"

The woman nods and smiles and ushers Mum towards two doors. One says *Laddies* and the other says *Lassies*. We're definitely not in North London now...

As Mum bustles off, shyness crashes into my chest like a punch. Automatically, I reach for my mobile – but of course with no signal, all I'm going to get is sniggers from the boy opposite if I pretend to check stuff on it.

So at first I act like I'm terribly interested in what's inside Mum's folder, taking out the Wilderwood Hall paperwork with trembling fingers. Fanning out the A4 sheets, I already know that the only one worth looking at is the floor plan of the building, which hides the fact that it's a broken-down antique dump and instead shows the basic layout, with the building as an L-shape.

The main house is the longer part of the L. On the ground floor is a huge entrance hall – the poshly named "vestibule" – and four equally huge stately rooms (which are a state in real life, Mum says). Directly above those, on the first floor, are six shabby-and-not-chic bedrooms. That – all of that, amazingly – will be "our" part of Wilderwood Hall when it's renovated.

The shorter part of the L is the East Wing, with the original Edwardian kitchens and pantries and stuff on the bottom, and the servants' quarters above. Mum says we're going to be more or less camping out in the servants' quarters for now, since that's the least wrecked part of the house. Later, when *it's* renovated, it'll be where our family and friends stay when they visit.

Not forgetting the bands who'll come to use the

recording studio RJ is having built in the old stable block.

And that, of course, is Mum and RJ's Shiny New Plan. RJ will rent out the studios and produce music here, and bands will not only stay, but they can use the house and gardens for photo shoots and videos. That's the side of the business *Mum* will run, since she's had loads of experience of that kind of thing in her old job.

And while Mum and RJ are busy with all of that, I'll be in one or another of these random rooms, staring into space. . .

Speaking of staring, I've had my eyes glued to these sheets of paper for for ever, and Mum's *still* not back. What now?

I glance around, and see that there're a few newspapers and magazines stuffed in a rack by the door. If I lean over, I can just about reach for one. . . And amazingly, the first thing I see is *not* a *Woman's Weekly* from 1972, which I'd kind of expected 'cause of the decor in this place. It's actually a lot more current; it's this week's copy of *Heat*. I grab it, welcoming the distraction.

How old does he look? I wonder, as I speed-flick past an article about a bloke from a reality show who has teeth so bleached they must glow in the dark.

I'm not thinking about the reality star, of course; it's the café's only other customer who's on my mind.

I risk a quick glance; the boy is leaning over, scratching behind the ear of one of the dogs. I notice a couple of thin, plaited leather bands tied around his skinny wrist. Those, along with the messy, fair hair and faded, worn jeans make him look more like a surfer boy from sunny Cornwall than a country "laddie" stuck in the deepest, darkest chilly Highlands of Scotland.

I reckon he's about my age, or maybe a year older? He's bound to be at Glenmill High, I realize. It's no wild guess, since that's the only secondary school for miles around, not counting some boarding school further north, somewhere even *more* remote from where we are. Both schools pinged up when I was googling the area. Out of the two of them, I guess I should be glad that Glenmill's where I'll be headed in two weeks' time, at the end of the holidays. But "glad" is not a word I feel like using about anything these days. . .

At that thought, I suddenly feel a sharp pang of longing for everything about my old school, and quickly drop my eyes back down towards the table, pretending to scan the pages of the magazine so no one can see the tears prickling my eyes.

The clamour of different accents; the terrible guess-what-meat-it's-supposed-to-be lunches; the rush to get the best benches at break time; my best friend Shaniya. How weird to think that she and the rest of the girls we hang out with will be doing the bench rush without me. Will they sit there with their crisps and energy bars and talk about me and my new life? Or will they forget me quick as—

Hold on. My fingers stop blindly flipping the pages and I backtrack to something that surprises me so much I forget to breathe.

"So the bad news is there's no wifi, but the good news is they do have *these*," says Mum, plonking a tray down on the table, laden with our drinks – and two Tunnock's Teacakes.

I say nothing, but just gaze up at her in shock.

"Wow, Ellis," says Mum as she pulls out the nearest chair and sits beside me. "I have never seen you less excited about your favourite-ever biscuit. Are you OK?"

I'm pretty much the *opposite* of OK, as Mum can clearly tell.

"I think I can guess what Shaniya put on Instagram," I say, moving the magazine around so Mum can see.

Her hand stops in mid-air, mid-reach for the teapot. She gasps.

'Cause there – on pages 19–20 of *Heat* – is Mum, in a series of sneaked photos. Taken on a long lens, she and an adoring RJ are seen milling around, kissing, hugging in their happy bubble (i.e., *before* they knew the photographer had them in his sights).

"No way! Listen to this: *Indie rock veteran RJ Johnstone stunned fans with his secret marriage to a mystery woman.*" Mum reads out the blurb that accompanies the images. The corny, dramatic words make her burst out laughing in that deep, throaty way of hers. The ancient waitress and the boy in the corner immediately stare over at us. They're probably wondering how such a tiny, pretty person can have such a dirty-sounding cackle. (Yep, it was another reason RJ fell for Mum.)

"Oh, good grief! Have you checked *this* one out?" Mum exclaims, and taps her finger on the photo at the bottom of the page. A photo of a familiar-looking girl in a lacy white top and skinny jeans, clutching a drooping bunch of flowers.

Yep, it's me, snapped being sick over the side of the boat. At least – thank you thank you thank you – my long brown hair hides my face. Now just *please* don't let Mum read out the caption that goes with it.

"What's this? *Oops! A boozy bridesmaid mars the rock 'n' roll wedding of White Star Line's RJ*," she says in a voice that's a little too loud for my liking. "As if! You're a seasick thirteen-year-old, that's all! Can't they get their facts right?"

(Whirl, tilt, shift.)

I've had exactly the right amount of travel-sickness pills today, and have so far survived the epic ten-hour drive here with only a sense of dread and not the faintest hint of queasiness. But now my head is swirling, and despite sitting down, I feel like the ground is dipping and moving beneath me.

"Ellis? Are you all right?" says Mum, placing her slim, cool hand on my forehead, instantly concerned. She's been really protective of me since my freak-out on the boat last week. But I guess she's always protective of me, anytime I've had one.

"Listen, Mum, can we just go?" I plead.

Urgh, my obvious desperation lands us *more* stares from the waitress, the boy, and even the dogs.

"Sure – of course," she says, getting up from the chair. "Let me just pay for this and ask the waitress for directions to Wilderwood. OK?"

"OK," I mutter, and get unsteadily to my feet. There's a window directly behind me, and if I turn to look out of it, I won't have to see our untouched snacks and anyone who happens to be staring over.

Instead, I can take in the uninspiring view of the main street of Glenmill – except for the fact that it's blocked by a flashy, big Range Rover. The funny thing is, it takes me a second to remember that the stupidly expensive, bulky car is *ours*. It was RJ's present to Mum before he left, since he didn't think our old, tiny Fiat would make it as far as the end of our road back in North London, never mind all the way up to Scotland.

It's also a *guilt* present, obviously, since the band's promo tour of Europe and beyond got moved forward by a fortnight and he had to leave us to fend for ourselves here in Nowheresville. . .

"Uh, hi," says a voice right beside me. Oh; it's the boy. Nerves kick in and my breathing does its panic dance – shallow and fast.

Still, up this close, I can't help noticing three things about him: he's a little shorter than me (plenty of people are); round his neck is a leather cord necklace that matches the bands around his wrist; and his eyes are small and dark ... darker than you'd expect, considering the lightness of his hair. They remind me of an animal's eyes. No, a *bird's*. They are definitely bird-like. In fact, he's staring at me like I'm a worm he's sizing up for dinner.

"So you're the new owners of Wilderwood?" he asks me straight out.

"I suppose so," I mumble in reply, though I can't say I've thought of the mansion that way. It's RJ's, after all.

"Wow, *you're* brave," the boy grins. "What did you think when you first saw the state it's in?"

"I – I haven't." I stumble over my words. "I mean, I've never been."

Neither has RJ. He bought Wilderwood Hall online, like book or a kettle or something. How crazy is that? I remember Mum telling me I had to do proper planning and research about my history project on the suffragettes, and yet in the time she and RJ have been together they've made every huge decision on the spur of the moment, like it's madly romantic instead of just plain mad.

"Wow," the boy says, and grins again. "Well, that's it over there. See?"

I look where he's pointing, expecting to see a random big building. But all that's in my line of vision is an untidy terrace of ancient, tiny houses on the other side of the street.

"Where?" I ask, confused.

"In the distance," says the boy. "You can only really see a bit of the East Wing."

Then I get it; above the chimney stacks, distant treetops sway in the wind. And visible in a gap in the trees is one pointed gable, with two small windows in it. Funnily enough, those windows look a little . . . well, a little like *eyes*. Glinting eyes that seem to be staring, staring across woodland, fields, rooftops, past soaring crows and skidding clouds. Staring past all that – straight at *me*.

With a whoosh and a rush, everything tips to one side, and I slip and sink into cool darkness. . .

When I wake, it's like coming up for air.

I rise from my sleepy depths and blink at the light streaming through the bare window. The room's walls are a faded pale blue ... that and the white duvet and fluffy pillows piled on the big bed make me feel as if I'm bobbing in frothy white horses in some faraway salty sea.

And bobbing beside me – on a fat pillow – is a Tunnock's Teacake, in its shiny wrapper. Smiling at Mum's jokey gesture, I take a couple of slow, deep breaths, and try to place myself.

The bed, the chest of drawers, the soft, fluffy rug on the rough wooden floorboards ... they're Mum's, but this isn't our cosy old flat. I'm in a rough-and-ready room on the first floor of the East Wing of Wilderwood Hall.

A glint of light on glass draws my gaze to the two framed photos propped up on the chest of drawers. One is of Mum cuddling me, aged three, the two of us damp and sandy after a dip in the sea, and now all bundled in a big towel on the beach. The other is Mum's favourite image from the wedding. It's a close-up of her hand resting in RJ's, the matching white star tattoos visible on each of their wrists.

Was it only two weeks ago since Mum and RJ got married? Time seems to be so ... so *stretchy* lately. Since RJ rolled into our world and sent it spinning in a different direction, I mean.

Wonder how early or late it is? I think and glance at my watch. Ten thirty? I've been asleep for hours and hours and *hours*... I mean, I remember Mum making me lie down for a nap on her bed as soon as the removal guys had set it up and she'd put the sheet and duvet and stuff on it.

Obviously, I must've slept through the rest of Day One at Wilderwood Hall. I slept though the furniture being clanked and thunked up the back stairs and shifted into the various rooms of the first-floor servants' quarters. So that means I also slept my way through the Tesco grocery delivery, the planned evening explore of the house and gardens with Mum, the whole, long night, in fact.

Swinging my legs out of the bed, I realize I'm still in yesterday's leggings and T-shirt. I spot my kicked-off trainers on the floor and shove my feet into them, since the bare floor's bound to be a girl trap of rubble, nails and splinters.

Up next: eat the Tunnock's Teacake (I'm starving), and go see what Day Two in Wilderwood Hall has in store. Of course, the first thing to do is search out my mother. And to find her, all I have to do is follow the sound of singing.

Mum's voice is faint, but I easily recognize the tune: White Star Line's "Turn the Corner". Even though he wrote it, RJ told Mum he thinks of it as "their" song. First, because the video shoot Mum and RJ met on was for that particular single. Second, 'cause RJ claims that the track was like some supernatural happening – he says it's as if he wrote the lyrics for Mum, before they'd ever set eyes on each other...

Pulling on a baggy old jumper I find on the floor, I peek out of the bedroom and find myself in a long corridor, peppered with doors. Looking left, towards one the end of the corridor, I can see a large doorway opening on to a set of plain stone stairs. That must lead down to the back door we came in through yesterday afternoon. The servants' entrance. And if I turn my head right – towards the other end of the corridor and the distant sound of singing – I can see a heavy, panelled door propped open with a cardboard packing box.

I walk towards it, knowing it must take me through into the main house. Downstairs, I remember from the floor plans, there's a passage that links the kitchens to the grand reception rooms, but *this* has to be the route the servants would have taken if they'd been needed by the master or mistress upstairs.

"... *And when your world isn't turning, and your path leads nowhere* ..."

Following Mum's lilting, carefree voice, I step through the doorway, and find myself on the wide, sun-filled, first-floor landing of Wilderwood Hall proper. Flutters of curiosity fill my chest, even though this strange house feels so far from home. So little like *my* home.

"... *Don't be scared, keep on walking* ..."

And I *am* walking, walking quickly past six

huge empty bedrooms, plaster fallen from walls, patches of ceiling languishing on floors, all their vast windows gazing out on to the wild Wilderwood grounds. More doors, closed doors, are on the opposite side of the landing from them. Cupboards? Bathrooms? I'll investigate later; I'm at the top of the yawningly wide, sweeping set of stairs now and want to find Mum.

"... *Turn the corner, I'll be there* ..."

Quickly, I trot down the steps towards an entrance hall – the "vestibule", obviously – that's so vast our entire flat back in London could fit in it. And the double front door; it looks wide enough to drive our new *car* through, if it was open.

"... *Turn the corner* ..."

I hurry across the echoing space, across the chipped cream-and-black tiles of the floor, singing the echoing part to the chorus, the part White Star Line's drummer usually takes.

"... *There I'll stand* ..."

"Ha!" Mum laughs delightedly as I hurtle into an enormous room with equally spectacular amounts of ornate mouldings and *actual* mould on the walls.

She's wearing old boyfriend jeans and her favourite pink Arran knit jumper. Her blonde-white hair is piled up on top of her head with a pencil stuffed in it, holding it all in place. Against one wall is a bunch of big boards, filled with sketches and designs and swatches of paint and fabric. On the dusty but lavish mantelpiece sits Mum's iPod dock, and White Star Line's single – "Turn the Corner" – is blasting from the travel speaker.

"*Turn the corner,*" Mum carries on with the chorus, arms now outstretched, doing RJ's line.

"*Take my hand,*" I sing, jokily holding my hand out to Mum. She grabs it, even though it's a bit sticky with chocolate and marshmallow gloop.

"*Turn the corner.*" Mum pulls me to her.

"*Don't be scared,*" I sing, mock sincere.

"*Turn the corner.*" Mum tilts her head, stares lovingly at me.

"*I'll be THERE!!*" I do that last bit in a dumb, over-the-top, operatic voice, and we both fall about laughing.

Then Mum lets go long enough to walk across to the fireplace and turn the volume down on the next track so we can hear each other talk.

In that tiny moment alone, I gaze around at the echoing, tatty room and my spirits sink again. What's Mum done taking us – dragging *me* – here?

"What made you stick that song on?" I ask her. "Missing your husband, Mrs Johnstone?"

My words are jagged with a hint of sarcasm. I can't help it.

"'Mrs Johnstone'. . . Ha! When will I get used to that?" Mum laughs, blissfully unaware of my barbed tone.

It's funny to think this is now Mum's third surname. She started out as Sadie Price, was very, very briefly Sadie Harper (when she married my dad), and now she's Sadie Johnstone. There are still plenty of Prices in our family – Granny and Uncle Ben and his family, who all emigrated to Australia – but now I'm the only one called Harper, since my dad doesn't count. That suddenly feels a lot like lonely. . .

"Anyway, yes, I'm missing RJ, but there's plenty to be getting busy with here!" Mum replies, spinning around in her white Converse trainers, as happy with the prospect of doing up this dump as a little kid being locked inside Legoland for the night.

I don't join in with the spinning; instead I stare some more at the state of the broken-down room, and think that it'll be a long, long time before Mum can get busy with details like paint and fabric. And it's just as well RJ is away working; camping out in the servants' quarters isn't exactly rock 'n' roll, is it? Plus I get Mum all to myself for just that little bit longer. We might be in the wrong place, but if I try really hard, maybe I can make-believe that it's just me and her against the world, same as it's always been. . .

"Anyway, enough of the house. How are you feeling?" Mum asks as she twirls her way over to the floor-to-ceiling, rotting French windows and pushes them – with a struggle – wide open.

"Better," I tell her. "Maybe I just needed a good sleep."

To be honest, I haven't slept well for weeks, with the upheaval of Mum and RJ and their whirlwind romance. Though, when I think of it, it's been longer than that. I haven't slept well for months, really.

"Good, I'm glad!" Mum smiles, stepping out on to the terrace. "You must have been exhausted after yesterday's drama, Ellis."

"Mum, it was hardly a drama," I say, following her and crossing my arms against the brisk, chilly Scottish wind that's penetrating my layers of clothes. "I was only out for a couple of minutes."

"A couple of minutes too long for my liking!"

Mum replies, patting my hand. "I still think I should've taken you to the nearest hospital to get you checked over. I know you've had your funny moments before, but this felt different."

"The lady in the café said that would've been two hours' drive away, though," I remind her.

"Hmm. Well, hopefully she's right, and you're just low on iron."

As I came round yesterday, I'd heard the elderly café waitress tell Mum that both her granddaughters had taken "turns" like this. "Some girls can be prone to it at this age. Anaemia, that is. They grow so fast, you see, and this young lass of yours is certainly big."

I'm "big". Urgh. I think everyone thought I'd groaned because I was in pain, but it was the awfulness of that description that hurt me most.

And then things got worse; I was staring up at Mum, the waitress and two inquisitive dogs ... but where was the bird-eyed boy? All of a sudden, it dawned on me that my head was in his *lap*, and I scrabbled to my feet quicker than the time Shaniya told me a giant spider had dropped from the ceiling on to my shoulder. (It was a small leaf. Shaniya's idea of a joke; well, it got a big laugh from everyone, except me, with my famous "sense-of-humour failure" as Shaniya calls it.)

"I'll be fine. I'll google it, and find out what foods I should be eating," I assure Mum.

"Well, you won't be able to do THAT till we get the engineer out to fix our internet connection. And I'm not sure how dependable the electrics are ... someone's coming to look at those soon, as well as the roofer and builder and plumber..." Mum's voice trails off as she pulls her mobile out of her back pocket and checks her list of whos, whats and whens that'll make the Shiny New Project start to take shape.

While she's momentarily frowning at her phone, I take a minute to gaze around at the grounds. When we arrived yesterday, Mum drove us – in drizzle – through tall, rusted, wedged-open gates, up the driveway, past the grand main entrance and on round to the back door, i.e., the servants' entrance. The drizzle fuzzed up our view, and I was feeling too fuzzed-up inside to be curious. As for Mum, as soon as she saw the removal van already parked up and waiting for us, that was all she could focus on.

"Hmm ... I'll be back in a sec, Ellis," Mum says

absent-mindedly. "I just want to see if I can get a signal from anywhere upstairs."

As she turns to go, in the corner of my eye I see the faintest flash of light glimmer, coming from the direction of the garden. I give an involuntary shiver.

"Feeling funny again, babes?" Mum asks, pausing when she spots that tiny movement of mine, the way mothers do.

And as her daughter, I'm pretty sure she's worried that my "turn" had nothing to do with iron or lack of it and everything to do with my "waves" getting worse.

"I'm just a bit cold," I say quickly. I guess the glimmer must've been a weak gleam of sunshine glinting off something.

"Come on inside, then," says Mum, ushering me to follow her.

"In a minute," I tell her. To be honest, I suddenly don't feel like doing every little thing Mum says. I did the big stuff, like letting her move us here, didn't I? That seems like plenty.

Mum frowns, but leaves me to myself. Maybe she's hoping that the healthy Highland air, the bracing breeze of it, will whip away any traces of anxiety. Same as maybe she's hoping I'll take one look at all the space – the endless space – we have here compared to our gardenless third-floor flat on our busy street in London and fall in love with Wilderwood as much as *she's* fallen in love with RJ.

It's not going to happen, of course. Wilderwood isn't some wonderland. Just look at the garden directly in front of the terrace; it must have been very grand once upon a time, laid out in four squares of planting. But now the ornamental hedges are overgrown and snarly, and the squares are empty of elegant roses and lilies and rampant with enthusiastic weeds instead.

Beyond that, a vast apron of long grass – dotted with trees and shrubs – extends to the perimeter stone wall. And beyond *that*, endless fir trees stand shoulder to shoulder, like a dense, living fence.

With a shudder, I decide to move on, to walk around the outside of the house and get my bearings. So I let the moss-covered paving stones take me along the front of the house, past more long, dirty, sometimes broken windows. Finally, I come to the corner of the building, the corner of the L. And it's here that I notice a large, lumpen tangle of ivy in the garden, way taller than me and spread wide. What's it covering? Has it grown over years – decades? –

and ended up smothering some shrubs growing there? Or covered an old garden shed, maybe?

More interestingly, beyond the ivy jungle I can now see part of the driveway, snaking down to meet the tiny single-track road that leads to the village.

The village! If I'm facing in the direction of Glenmill, that means the windows I saw from the Cairn Café – they *have* to be directly above me, in the East Wing; the shorter part of the L. I flip around and look up at the rooms above the kitchens – but I'm too close to the building to see properly.

Taking a step back, and another, and another, I scan the upper floor.

And now I get a better view. Just like you'd expect, the roof of the servants' quarters is pretty plain, except for one pair of windows that have a decorative triangle of stone above them, echoing the style of the main house frontage.

Yes; *they're* the windows that seemed like eerily staring eyes yesterday. But today, from this angle, they're plain and blank. Simple glass in old wooden frames, letting light into a dusty, musty room.

Reassured, and feeling a bit silly, I take *another* step back, and—

Ow!

I've just been kicked, *hard*, in the back of both knees.

I'm crumpling, tumbling, balance shot and arms flailing to catch hold of something, anything.

And in that split second of sinking, I feel like Alice tumbling into the rabbit hole, bottle-green ivy closing in over me...

My wrists still ache from being wrenched. Mr Fraser
sees me rubbing them and apologizes again.

"Sorry, sweetheart," he says, embarrassment
reddening his already ruddy cheeks. "Didn't mean
to be so rough."

Mum hands him a mug of tea and quickly sets
him straight. "Oh, please don't apologize! If you
hadn't grabbed Ellis when you did, she could've
cracked her head really badly."

"Yes, thanks," I mumble shyly, and hide my red
wrists behind my back. "I didn't know the fountain
was there, hidden under all that ivy."

I'm especially shy because Mr Fraser isn't alone.
His son has come with him. His scruffy-haired,

bird-eyed teenage son who saw me faint in the café yesterday, and stagger backwards – like a Mr Bean wannabe – into a disused pond this morning. Great. I'm so used to being known as an awkward, clumsy "beanpole" at school in London, and now it seems like I'll be known for that here too, once I start at Glenmill High. . .

"Funny the secrets you come across around an old place like this," says Mr Fraser, shuffling his work boots on the floorboards of what was, once upon a time, the grand dining room of Wilderwood Hall. "Just glad me and Cameron came around the corner when we did."

"Cam." His son mumbles a correction to his name.

While I'd stood brushing ivy leaves out of my hair and off of my jumper, Mr Fraser and his son – *Cam* – had begun tugging roughly at the strands of vines, till the stone fountain began to reveal itself. They'd seemed pretty impressed at uncovering a chunk of the house's history. All *I* saw was a hunk of granite that had (shamefully) tripped me up while I wasn't looking.

"Exactly!" Mum says enthusiastically. "Anyway, talking about things you come across in an old place

like this, wait till you see what's in the kitchen. . .
Come and take a look."

At first I think that Mum's talking about the titchy kitchen I vaguely looked in yesterday upstairs in the servants' quarters, the one that's ugly and basic and falling to pieces. But instead she waves us all out of the dining room, along the wide corridor, till we come to a simpler passageway on our left. From the position of it, I guess that it must lead through to the original kitchen in the East Wing.

"So, this place is what – about a hundred years old?" I hear Mr Fraser ask, as he strides along the cool grey flagstones, past doors painted a chipped and faded gloss green.

Cam is behind me, which is pretty awkward. Or unnerving. Or maybe a mix of both. He's probably looking at how tall and gangly I am and wondering how I can be related to such a tiny, pretty person as my mum. Meanwhile, I'm wondering where his dogs are, but I'm not about to ask him, no way.

"It's Edwardian, built in 1911, according to the deeds," Mum chats easily as she leads the way. "The original owner was apparently a Mr Richards, from London. Do you happen to know anything else about Wilderwood?"

"Not much, but then we only moved to Glenmill from Glasgow a couple of years back," says Mr Fraser.

OK, so bang goes my theory about everyone in Glenmill having lived here for ever. Still, it might not apply to Cam Fraser and his family, but I bet it goes for everyone else, like the ancient waitress in the Cairn Café.

"Oh, really? So you're not quite up to speed with all the local history – or gossip, then?" Mum jokes, forgetting for a second who she's married to, and the fact that *we* might end up being the local gossip, if we're not already.

Mr Fraser laughs, charmed by Mum, I can tell.

"All I *did* hear was that it sat empty for decades," he tells her, "till some hippy bloke bought it in the 1970s, I think it was, with a view to doing it up. He only lived in a few of the smaller rooms upstairs in this wing, apparently. Never had the money to do up the main house, I don't think."

"Well, it *is* quite a project, but we're looking forward to it," says Mum. "Anyway, here we are. What do you reckon to this, Ellis?"

I go to follow Mum and Mr Fraser into the large, echoing room, which is completely empty, apart from a mammoth black cooking range.

But as I put my hand on the door frame, something happens. A sudden storm of noise hits me. Chatter. Clattering. A rush of water. A metallic-sounding bell ring-a-dinging incessantly. Then someone is holding my elbow – and I don't want them to.

"Ellis? Ellis, honey?"

Mum's voice cuts through the cacophony and it melts away as fast as it came, leaving me feeling clammy and crazy around the edges. I pull my elbow away from what I realize is Cam's hand. He's staring at me with those sharp eyes of his, like he's taking in every detail so he can tell his friends in the village all about me, all about us, later.

I'm suddenly angry as well as embarrassed and confused. What's Cam even doing here, anyway? *Did* he tag along with his dad 'cause he's sussed who Mum's married to? The estate agent was meant to be keeping it a secret. Still, stuff gets out – look at the photos in *Heat*. Except… Except maybe I left the magazine open on the tartan-covered table yesterday and blew the secret myself?

"I – I'm OK. I'm just a bit cold," I say directly to Mum, pretending my hesitation is all to do with temperature and nothing to do with strange sounds in my head. (Maybe I *did* bump it in the fountain before Mr Fraser pulled me free. Or I could've got whiplash. That can make you feel pretty weird, can't it?)

Mum frowns, trying to use her parental intuition to figure out if I'm fibbing or not. Maybe I should get out of here, before the waves rush in...

"I'm just going to get changed into something warmer," I say, pointing my thumb in the direction of the servants' quarters upstairs. "Where's my stuff?"

"Oh, I chose a really nice room for you, with the best views. The removal men put all your furniture and bags and boxes in already, so you'll find it OK," says Mum. "And if you go through the big door in the passageway behind you, it'll take you straight to the back stairs, and save you trailing through the main house again."

I nod and smile (or as close as I can manage) and turn to leave so Mum and Mr Fraser can discuss scaffolding and roof joists and damp courses in peace.

"Excuse me," I mumble at Cam, and slither past him, pulling open the nearest heavy door, hoping madly it's the right one and that I don't have to backtrack. Luckily, it is, and I'm grateful for the cool bite of air on my hot cheeks as I stamp up the grey stone steps of the stairwell.

What exactly happened back there in the kitchens? I can't feel any bumps on the back of my head so I'm not sure if I can blame concussion. Maybe I'm just over-imaginative. That's what Granny called me, after I'd Skyped to tell her I'd won an inter-school poetry competition last term. Granny sat there in the Sydney morning sunshine and listened as I read out my poem about refugees, then told me I'd "always been an over-imaginative child". I'd beamed and said thank you, but as soon as I'd finished the call, I'd wondered if it actually was a compliment. I'm never very sure with Granny; she's not a cuddly kind of grandmother – though I guess it's hard to cuddle someone when they live more than nine thousand miles away. But maybe Granny has a point. Maybe I *am* over-imaginative, if I'm hearing things that aren't even there. . .

I shake those thoughts from my head as I reach the vaguely familiar territory of the servants' quarters' corridor and start to hunt around for whichever room Mum's chosen for me. Nope, not here – Mum's turned this into a temporary living room, with our sofa and TV from London looking strangely at home. (More at home than I look, I bet.)

And not here; I've found myself back in Mum's bedroom, where I spent the night. The next door leads to the nasty '70s kitchenette; next to *that* is the bathroom (complete with original, and stained, Edwardian sink and loo, with a modern-ish shower stuffed in a corner). This next room is set up with a desk and more mood boards and is obviously Mum's nerve centre for the Shiny New Project.

All that's left are two doors facing each other at the end of the corridor, the end nearest the linking entrance to the main house. The first door I stick my head around reveals a dreary little space, with a small, cobweb-curtained window. It's obviously destined to be the spare room; our old futon is plonked in the middle of it, folded flat and waiting to be assembled. So I turn and cross the corridor to the only room remaining.

It's not a good start – I put my hand out to grab a doorknob but there isn't one. I stand back and check out the door in front of me; where a brass lock should be there's just a rectangular grooved outline, and some dents in the wood as if someone once hacked the whole thing off with a hammer.

And the old green paint ... it's not just faded and chipped like the other doors along the corridor, it's also blistered and blackened on the bottom half.

With a shiver, I push the battered door open and reluctantly step inside – and find myself in a room flooded with light. It's because of the pair of windows directly in front of me. They're not huge, but they're big enough to let sunbeams spill across the bed, chest of drawers and piles of boxes I last saw when I packed up my room back in London, back home. It's not till I walk over to the windows, till I've looked out at the view of the driveway, the swaying trees, the glimpse of buildings in the village beyond that I realize where I am.

I'm here. In the room with eyes. Ha! It looked so eerie from afar, and yet close up ... it's so different.

I flip around and lean against the slim piece of wall between both windows and survey my new room. And a glimmer of hope fills my heart like a weak shaft of sunlight peeking through a skyful of lurking grey clouds.

You know, so far I've been *beyond* unimpressed by the echoing, elderly building site that Wilderwood is. But if I block that from my mind, I think I might come to like this one small part of it. My room at our old flat was at the front of our block, and overlooked by offices on the other side of the road. It was always in shadow. Not like this place, where I can see dust motes twirling gently in the air, air light with brightness streaming in from outside.

And the quiet ... ! There's no roar of cars and vans, no bleeping of horns and meeping of reversing lorries. There's no sound at all. Apart from a sort of low-level buzzing, or humming, that's gently vibrating somewhere.

Has Mr Fraser already begun drilling something downstairs? I twist around and put my ear right against the wall.

And pull it away almost immediately.

It's voices. Voices whispering, whispering in the walls...

5

It's a miracle. I *can* get a signal in my room. Well, bizarrely, after moving around – including a stint standing (shaking) on my bed with my mobile held above my head – I've found the best place to get any bars is sitting hunched down on the floor by the door.

And miracle number two: Shaniya has forgiven me enough to talk to me.

"What did the voices say?" asks Shaniya. "WE ARE COMING FOR YOU, MWAH HA HA!"

Shaniya is always making jokes. I guess that's what makes our friendship work – she's loud and fierce and funny, and I'm ... not. People say opposites attract, don't they? Though sometimes we don't get along. In Shaniya's case, when I have one of my sense-of-humour failures. Or do stuff like not invite her to my mum's star-studded wedding.

"No," I reply, tucking my baggy jumper over my knees and turning myself into a woolly package. "I couldn't make out actual words. It was more like . . . like I was hearing some conversation in another room."

I'd only heard the whisperings for a few seconds, but I'd been so freaked out by them I'd wanted to run downstairs and beg Mum to drive us back to our flat in London straight away. But that wasn't going to work, not when Mum had already given up the lease on our old place and handed in the keys. And even if it *was* possible, I couldn't physically ask her anyway; not when – as I could see out of the window – she was with Mr Fraser, excitedly pointing at bits of broken-down building, with Cam trailing uselessly behind them.

So my second-best option was to swallow my pride and call my best friend.

"Well, that's probably all it was, then! Gawd, you can be so dramatic sometimes, Ellis!" Shaniya laughs.

"I'm not trying to be dramatic," I protest, feeling

ripples of anxiety lap at my chest. "It's just that Wilderwood is really . . . *strange*. I don't know how I can ever get used to living here."

"What – you can never get used to living in a giant mansion with more rooms than your family could ever need?" Shaniya teases me.

OK, I got that wrong. Like I often get things wrong with her. And I understand – Shaniya lives in a small flat in a not-great estate and has to share a bedroom with her little sister, who's pretty severely autistic. I know that, and I always listen to her talk about what her home life's like and sympathize or try to help.

"I'm sorry," I say, flustered. "I didn't mean it to. . ."

I drift away, not sure what exactly I'm apologizing for but feeling bad for my friend anyway.

"Look I've got to go," says Shaniya. "Mum wants me. Talk to you later, yeah?"

"Yeah," I reply, but she's already gone.

And hearing the empty drone of nobody there, I crumple, feeling light years from home and so, so alone. Except I have Mum, of course. I take a deep breath, and try and steady myself.

I don't care whether Mum is peering down drains or talking toilets with Mr Fraser, I just want to be close to her right now. She might be small, but when I'm with her, I'm surrounded by her force field of love, and that's a pretty special place to be.

And once we're alone, I can tell her about the whisperings and the noises I've been hearing. Somehow, she'll make some kind of sense of it all, I know she will.

Scrambling to my feet, I pull the door open and aim for the back stairs.

But then I hear the crunch and roar of a vehicle on gravel, and through the window in the stairwell I see a white van – Mr Fraser's, presumably – drive off.

Perfect!

So it's back to just being me and Mum, and it'll be that way for a whole month, till RJ's back from his promotional tour with the band, I remind myself.

Even if I'm marooned in this strange new world, as long as me and Mum are together, I'll be OK.

First, of course, I have to find her, in this stupidly huge house.

"Mum?" I call out, thundering down the back stairs and opening the door to the warren of kitchen rooms. My heart pitter-patters as I walk over to the doorway of the room with the huge cooking range –

but everything is still, quiet as an empty church. Tentatively, I put my hand on the door frame, but there's only a reassuring silence.

Turning around, I follow the passageway that leads to the main house. When I came the other way earlier, with Cam right behind me, I was too frazzled to notice the hand-painted, beautifully neat gold lettering on each of the many dark green doors along here. *Servants' Hall*, *Cook's Rooms*, *Scullery*, *Larder*, *Pantry*. I turn the brass handle of each as I pass, but none opens. Rooms to be explored another time, when I get Mum to show me where the keys are.

And now I'm out in the main house, with four open doors off the wide corridor leading to what used to be the billiard room, the library, the drawing room and the dining room, and are now just cavernous spaces waiting for new life to be breathed into them.

"Mum?" I call out again, as I pad along, wondering where she is. And then I see her, past the staircase and in the vestibule. She's by the open front door, and from the way Mum's head is tilted to one side and her elbow sticks out, I can tell she's on her phone.

Practically skipping over to her, I wrap my hands around her waist, as glad as I ever have been to see my gorgeous mother.

But Mum does something she's never done before. She shrugs me off.

"Look – I've only *just* got a signal, Ellis, and I don't want to lose it. This is important, OK?" she practically snaps at me.

I don't know what to do, or how to react. Mum being like that towards me ... it makes me feel more like I'm losing my mind than I did when I heard the sounds that weren't there. With waves suddenly rushing in, I back off and run, running from the rising anxiety and running from Mum.

As I hurtle up the swoop of the main stairs, I listen out for her coming after me, or at least shouting her sorries. But she doesn't come, she doesn't call out.

Now on the first floor of Wilderwood Hall, I hurry past the blank and beat-up "grand" bedrooms, aiming for the panelled door near the far end of the landing that'll take me through to the East Wing, back to the servants' quarters and the sanctuary of my new bedroom.

But before I get there, I see brightness beaming

from the furthest-away "grand" bedroom. Its doorway faces the panelled one I'm headed for. My heart rate slows, and instead of turning left into the servants' quarters, as I'd planned, I turn right, drawn into the sunbeam room.

Because it's positioned at the corner of the building, it has these big, wide windows on two sides. I drift to the closest and see that it has views of the rooftops of nearby Glenmill – same as my room. The second overlooks the gardens, the driveway, the rusted, wedged-open iron gates, as well as the woods and the snow-capped mountains beyond.

Even with my head filled with muddle and misery, I can't help wondering who might have slept in this room, in the long-ago days when Wilderwood was alive with some fancy rich family and their hard-working staff.

Leaning against a wall that's powdery with old paint, I gaze around for clues, though there's nothing much to see apart from debris on the floor and a hole in the wall where a fireplace must've once stood.

Was this the master bedroom, for Mr Richards – the original landowner – and his wife? Probably not … it's too close to the servants' quarters for that. Then perhaps it was a guest room? Or a child's bedroom, or the nursery, maybe?

Then I hear something. A sound, a noise, that's enough to make my rambling thoughts grind to a halt. The noise isn't loud, but in the quiet of this empty room it stands out like a black crow in a snowstorm. It's a noise like the hissing of escaping gas or air. Or some distant, hazy voice that flits by on the radio, when you're trying to find the right station.

OK, OK, I *know* it's only the rush and fizz of my own pounding blood, but – dumbly – I try and listen in to the murmuring hiss, as if I'll somehow be able to decipher it.

Hold still. My breath still too. Tuning in. And then my stomach lurches. I just made out a word in the whisperings.

"Leave. . ."

It's a small voice. A child's.

"Leave, leave, leave. . ." I hear the ever-so-faint, scratchy voice repeat over and over again.

(Whirl, tilt, shift.)

6

Lurching unsteadily, I make it out of the room and on to the landing – and stop dead.

Directly in front of me is the connecting door to the servants' quarters. Two minutes ago, it was propped open with one of our packing boxes ... but now it's closed.

The cream-coloured paint of the door; it's glossy and new, I realize as I walk over to touch it in wonder. It's as new as the ivory wallpaper all the way down the landing, with its pretty pattern of something I think might be honeysuckle. And my feet ... my scruffy trainers are standing on something that shouldn't be there.

With my breath caught in my throat, I stare

down at an ornately patterned long runner of carpet that covers the landing's highly polished dark floorboards.

"*LEAVE!*" I hear a child's voice screech this time.

The voice is coming from behind me in the room, and – completely rigid with shock – I don't know what to do or what to think.

"All right, I'm leaving, I'm leaving. . ." another voice grumbles in a Scottish accent, and I turn to see a teenage girl coming out of the bedroom behind me, carrying a heavy-looking coal scuttle.

She's wearing the long black dress and the white apron and cap of a servant. She's small and scrawny and doesn't look strong enough to be carrying anything so bulky as that scuttle.

But here's the most important thing about her: she can't be real. I mean, there was no one and *nothing* in that room just now – except for the whisperings in the walls.

Or maybe it's *me* who isn't real. . .

The girl's just passed so close to me that our shoulders nearly touched, and yet it's as if I'm invisible. She doesn't react to me at all – she only pauses long enough to tuck a stray sweaty curl of brown hair behind her ear and sigh unhappily.

And now I watch with breath-held, numb curiosity as the servant girl tugs desperately at the handle of a stiff door in the wall just along from me. It's one of those I thought must lead to old storage cupboards when I walked past them earlier. The muscles in her jaw clench as the door handle resists her grip, or maybe it's the high-pitched, bad-tempered squalling of the child back in the bedroom that's causing her stress.

"*Ahhhhhhhhhhhhh!*"

"Shush that shouting, Master Archibald!" a stern voice now pipes up from the direction of the staircase I hurried up only a few minutes ago.

Frozen as a chill marble statue, I watch horrified as a young woman appears at the top of the stairwell and shuffles daintily along the landing at high speed towards me, only the tips of her black shoes visible under her long grey skirt. She is looking in my direction. I am clearly here.

But it's clear she can't see me either.

And now the grumbling servant girl gives the reluctant door a final, frantic tug and it opens outwards. She hurriedly goes inside, pulling the door closed behind her, brass scuttle clanking.

With the screeching of the child – the *boy* –

continuing, the young woman lifts her skirts and breaks into as much of a run as her clothing will allow her.

"Stop that noise this instant, Master Archibald – you'll disturb your mamma!" she calls out.

She is so close that I can see the cameo brooch at the high neck of her stiff blouse, the pale silhouette of a girl's face on a terracotta background.

As the woman rustles by me and into the bedroom, I gasp at the small brush of air, the proof of her living, breathing real self.

And as she disappears into the room, the scent of a flowery perfume lingers in her wake.

"But Miss Matilda!" I hear the boy in the bedroom whine. "Flora banged into me and—"

"And you're tittle-tattling on the girl again, Master Archibald. Now let her get on with her work and we'll get on with ours. I would like to hear you recite the alphabet again, please."

As the boy continues to moan and protest, I feel prickles of pins and needles in my hands and feet, as if I've been suspended in ice-cold water and I'm now warming my way back to life.

With a sudden surge of urgency and sureness, I know I need to get through to the servants' quarters.

I wrap my tingling fingers around the shiny brass doorknob and feel stupidly grateful as I hear and feel the clunk of the mechanism turn in my hand.

But in the split second before I step through to the other side, something makes me look left, up the long length of the landing. And I see the servant girl, peeking out of the tiniest crack in the cupboard door. Flora, the boy called her.

She is poised at the gap, listening to the griping and grizzling of the spoilt, troublesome little boy, and the telling off he's getting from the woman, who must be his governess.

But Flora isn't just listening; with eyes wide, she's watching too. Watching *me*. . .

7

I flatten myself, pressing my whole weight against the connecting door to keep the weirdness safely on the other side.

To stop it following me through to the reassuringly tatty, twenty-first-century servants' quarters.

Because in the here and now, still-unpacked boxes line the corridor – and the normality of that makes me almost giddy with relief.

Just so I'm absolutely sure that I'm definitely, positively, safely back in the present day, I turn my head left and get a glimpse inside the dusty, drab room where our old futon is plonked. At the sight of it, I get a flash of memory, an image of the moment I spilt blackcurrant juice on it, when I'd jumped at a "scary" moment in *Scooby-Doo* years ago.

More normality, I realize, picturing the faded stain that's still there, usually hidden by an artfully placed cushion. And if I turn my head to the right, I'm looking directly into "my" room. From this position – still star-shaped against the door through to the main house – I can't see much of it except for one plastic black bag of my belongings, which has been hastily dumped on the floor by the removal men and torn at the side. Some familiar pink, polka-dot fabric is poking through the tear, as if my pyjama bottoms are trying to make a run for it. . .

I can't believe I'm actually giggling, considering I'm quietly losing my mind. Though maybe getting hysterical is a symptom of going completely—

THUD!

The door thumps against my back and my heart practically gives out.

"Ellis? Ellis, are you there?" Mum's muffled voice calls out.

I let go of my breath like a deflating balloon.

"Yes – hold on!" I yelp, whipping myself around and pulling the door open.

The first-floor landing of the main house is – thankfully – just as it should be: scruffy, unloved and empty of everyone except my mother.

"What did you close the door for?" Mum asks.

"I didn't! It was—" I hesitate, noticing that Mum looks worried and tense. She's biting the inside of her mouth the way she always does when she's stressed. Usually that's to do with bills and rent and lack of money, but it's not as if Mum has to worry about stuff like that any more.

"What's wrong?" I ask her.

"Nothing," Mum says too quickly, too sharply. "Nothing's wrong. Look, I'm sorry about being short with you downstairs just now – there's just . . . just a lot to organize."

I don't get it. Everything about the house is an organizational nightmare, but Mum's been totally up for it. She was up for it when she strolled around the house with Mr Fraser just now, happily examining every crack, fault and disaster. It was all "exciting" first steps in the Shiny New Project.

What's happened in the last few minutes to change that?

"Who were you talking to on the phone?" I ask her, since that might hold the clue.

"It was … it was the internet provider. Boring stuff. Forget it."

We studied body language in Citizenship at school last term. Apparently, people can't look you in the eye when they're lying. Apparently, Mum is lying.

Why would she do that? She tells me everything. We tell each *other* everything. "Secrets aren't good for people," I remember Mum always saying. Has she conveniently forgotten that?

"You know, you don't look so well again, Ellis," says Mum, stepping away from her fib and closer to me. She puts her small, cool hand on my hot forehead. "You feel a bit clammy."

OK, now is the time to tell her what I saw – *who* I saw – out on the landing.

"I'm OK, I'm not sick," I insist. "It's this house; it's making me feel crazy. Just now I—"

Mum's phone begins to ring and her already pale face goes chalk white.

"Oh, I have to get this, Ellis…" she says, and walks hurriedly past me. I watch as she turns into her "office" – and closes the door behind her. I feel completely shut out.

Who is she speaking to? I pad over to the office

and try to listen in. For a couple of minutes, all I can make out is her uh-huhs and yeses and buts and occasional sighs, as the person at the other end of the call hogs the conversation. And it's hard to hear even that, since the panic waves are rushing in, and the blood is pounding and thundering in my ears.

I wish I could run away somewhere I feel safe. But that's nowhere in this house of many rooms. Not with all its visions and whisperings. . .

The grinning, hairy man is still squeezing and squeaking a corny Scottish folk tune out of his accordion.

"Oh, speed, bonnie boat, like a bird on the wing. . ."

The elderly waitress trills along to the ancient videotape as she comes over, then plonks a hot chocolate and Tunnock's Teacake down in front of me. Her name is Moira. After she properly introduced herself, she asked me my name and my mum's name, and seemed happy with that amount of information. Maybe she's saving nosier questions for later.

"Like I say, I don't have enough money," I tell her apologetically, spreading the few pence and bits of pocket fluff out on the plastic tartan tablecloth.

"Och, call it a welcome to the village 'freeb', dear," says Moira, the wrinkles on her face crinkling as she smiles.

I try a smile back, even if I'm not sure what she's on about.

"That is what you young folk call it, isn't it? A 'freeb'?"

"Oh, I think you mean freebie," I shyly correct her.

"Ha! I think some of the teenagers who come in here would be rolling their eyes if they heard me saying that!" Moira laughs.

"Like Cam?" I say, then wish I hadn't. I don't want her to think I'm remotely interested in the boy with the blackbird eyes.

"Yes, like Cam!" she says brightly. "I saw him when I was opening up earlier. He was taking himself off to the pool today, though how he can be bothered on a chilly day like today I don't know."

The pool ... there's a leisure centre here in the middle of nowhere?

"Anyway, it's lovely that Wilderwood will have a bit of life breathed back into it," Moira chatters on, gazing out of the window at the far-off watching windows of my new bedroom.

"Do you know much about its history?" I ask her, since she's obviously old enough and local enough to know the Hall better than the more newly arrived Mr Fraser.

"Not at all, dear – I only moved to the village a few months ago," she tells me. "My son and daughter-in-law moved here from Edinburgh and bought the old hotel down the road and this café. They persuaded me to come join them and help out here while they concentrate on the hotel."

Moira isn't a local resident either?

"All I know is that Wilderwood's sat empty for decades, withering away, like a doddery old duchess!" joked Moira. "Till you and your mum came along to rescue her in the nick of time, of course."

I quite like that she doesn't know about RJ, and I'm not about to tell her.

"Someone else tried to do it first," I tell her. "In the 1970s, a man bought it and lived in it on his own. We heard he couldn't afford to do it up and ... and he gave up, I think."

"Really? Ooh, that's interesting, isn't it? I wonder what—"

There's a sudden tinkle of the old-fashioned bell

above the café door, and two people dressed in hiking boots and fleeces come stomping in. And so Moira bustles off, leaving me with the sugary steam of the hot chocolate twirling under my nose, and my fingers already tugging the silver foil from the teacake.

How funny … it's just dawned on me that I've barely eaten since yesterday, when I had half a sandwich for lunch in a service station north of a pretty little town called Perth. Since then I've eaten nothing but a teacake for breakfast (served to me on Mum's pillow this morning). Rather than whiplash from my tumble, is *that* why I've been so light-headed? Why I've been feeling so strange? Hey, I've accidentally starved myself, and *that's* the reason I've started hearing and seeing things…

Relief floods through my chest as the first sip of hot chocolate warms me through. Now I'm glad that I left that note for Mum while she was on the phone and went for a walk, the nearest thing I could get to escaping. I'm even more glad that during my mooch through the grounds of Wilderwood, I came across the path that led over a stile, through an open, grassy field, and discovered it was a shortcut to the village of Glenmill.

And I'm particularly glad that I saw Moira waving at me through the plate glass window of the Cairn Café, while I sat – beginning to shiver – on a lone bench by the bus stop, wondering what to do with myself next. (Inbuilt shyness *nearly* made me pretend not to see her, but inbuilt politeness meant I couldn't allow myself to do that.)

And now, with Moira busy and bustling and no stray boys and dogs to stare at me, I get the chance to gaze properly around the steamy room. Apart from all the tartan and thistle corniness, there are quite a few framed black-and-white photos on the walls. The one closest to me is of the main street here, with the café looking much as it does now – though there's a date of *1963* scribbled in the corner of it.

Above that is a much older looking photo, of a shop this time, with a shopkeeper standing proudly outside it in a cap and long apron. There are children staring fascinated towards the camera, and from their clothes and bonnets, I'm guessing this picture was from Victorian or Edwardian times.

In fact … getting up and looking closer, I can see that the grocer's shop in the photo is what's now the Cairn Café.

I stand up to nosy at the next batch of framed prints. Here's a church, a tumbledown bridge, some mountains and a river. Maybe I'll be able to spot the modern-day versions of these old-time views once I get to know the area. After all, I've got nothing better to do than drift around the place, have I?

And this one; it looks fun ... a group of young boys in nothing but long johns seem to be taking turns to jump into a frothing cauldron of water in the middle of some woods. Some printed lettering underneath says "Linn o' Glenmill". Those kids who are waiting are in perfect focus, but the mid-jumpers are a blur, since exposure times on long-ago cameras took for ever.

This outdoor pool is carved into rock, and looks deep. I bet it's freezing, even on a hot day.

Hold on ... is this the pool Moira was talking about? Has Mr Fraser's son, Cam, headed for a wild swim there today, whether it's chilly or not?

Cramming the last chunk of teacake in my mouth, I lean over to drop the balled-up silver foil on to my table – and catch sight of a photo on the furthest-away wall.

Immediately, I begin to weave my way between the tables, screeching chairs out of the way. Because even from a distance, I've recognized the shape of the imposing double front door and steps in the image. And once I'm standing in front of the ornate but chipped frame, I pause to read the brass plaque on the bottom of it: *Wilderwood Hall, April 1912.*

My heart gives a little lurch at the sight of those etched words.

It lurches again as I lift my gaze to study the group of people standing posed on the steps.

People whose backs are straight, and whose faces are stern, just as the photographer urged them to be. "Hold still," I could imagining him shouting politely but firmly at the upstanding, finely dressed Master and Mistress of Wilderwood House, with their retinue of staff fanned around them in the monotone shades of servants' outfits.

Wealthy Mr and Mrs Richards, from London, in their relatively newly built, grand Scottish estate.

And now I stare, fascinated, at one face that's just a blur. One person didn't obey the photographer's orders, but that's because the person is only a small child. A little boy, by the look of it, though the bloomer style of his trousers would be considered a girl-style fashion nowadays. The blurred boy is holding the hand not of his mother, but of a tall young woman, with a cameo brooch at the high neck of her blouse. . .

No, no, no, NO!

Agitatedly, I scrabble in my pocket and find my phone. I need to take a photo of this portrait, so I can study it properly, so I can try to make sense of this when I'm back home, with Mum. I know I was a bit cross with her just now, but that doesn't matter; I just want to show her this picture and talk it over together and—

"Ellis? Oh, Ellis!" Moira calls over to me. "Can you be of help to this young lady?"

I hadn't noticed the jangly bell above the door tinkle again, or seen the new customer come in.

I hadn't heard the girl with the long red hair and beanie hat ask for a bottle of water and directions to where she was going next.

The girl is older than me, taller than me, but in a non-gawky way. She looks like a sulky supermodel on her way to a festival.

But behind her black-rimmed glasses I can see she's dark around the eyes, and looks exhausted, as if she and her rucksack have had a long, hard journey.

On the far side of the counter, Moira's face radiates smile lines and optimism.

On the near side of the counter, the girl's face is gaunt and tense.

I have no idea who she is, but from the way she's staring at me, it's as if . . . as if she *hates* me.

"She's looking for Wilderwood Hall, Ellis," Moira explains, aware of the sudden, awkward silence pulsating between us.

"It's my father's house," the girl says almost bitterly.

I hold tight to the nearest table, ready for the waves to roll in. . .

Sucking at sudoku. A deep love of Motown songs. A bizarre craving for Marmite with peanut butter on toast. Surprisingly similar childhoods in sleepy seaside towns. Virtually matching bluebird tattoos (on Mum's ankle, on RJ's shoulder).

In between takes for the video shoot of "Turn the Corner", Mum and RJ sat in the make-up room, hugging mugs of Earl Grey tea and chatting like instant old friends. The more they talked, the more coincidences popped up in the conversation, amazing and delighting them both. One particular coincidence that blew them away was the fact that they had daughters with such similar-sounding names: Ellis and Eloise.

I don't know the order the coincidences came in, but when Mum told me about them, I did wonder if this – the pretty pairing of Ellis & Eloise – might have tipped Mum and RJ over the edge into love... But hey, the reality isn't very pretty.

We're both crammed together in the wide front seat of Mr Fraser's big white van, Eloise's parka bunched up against my denim jacket. Eloise bites at her ultra-short purple-varnished nails, and neither of us says a word while Mr Fraser drives us from the café to Wilderwood. Cam's two sheepdogs, whose seats we've stolen, I think, are howling in the back.

My excuse for not talking is that my stomach, as usual, is churning from travel-sickness and anxiety, as the van jiggles and rocks first along the single-track road and now through the broken-down gates of the Wilderwood estate and on up the gravel driveway.

I don't know what Eloise's excuse for silence is; maybe travel-sickness too (didn't RJ once say something about that?) or maybe she's just sick at the sight of me, some stupid girl who's trying to steal her father away. All I do know is that she's said nothing to me apart from our initial, curt conversation back in the café, which ran along the lines of...

"Can you take me to see my dad?"

"You mean RJ?"

"Yes."

"Er, he's not at Wilderwood at the moment."

"Oh."

"Do you maybe want to speak to my mum?"

" . . . "

I'd taken that as a yes, since Eloise hadn't said no.

Guessing that my mobile wouldn't get reception, Moira the waitress then motioned for me to help myself to the café's landline. And so I'd been standing with the receiver pressed to my ear – desperately hoping Mum was located in some part of Wilderwood that had reception – when Mr Fraser popped into the café.

As I stood *willing* Mum to pick up (she didn't), Moira served Mr Fraser a takeaway coffee, found out he was heading back to Wilderwood with supplies he'd picked up, and arranged for him to take both me and Eloise home in his van.

"Well," says Mr Fraser finally, his voice sounding forced and uncomfortable. "Here we are, girls. . ."

The van crunches to a stop outside the back entrance to the house, and Mum – who must've seen or heard it approaching – comes stepping out of the doorway. She gives Mr Fraser a wave hello but comes straight over to the passenger side when she spots me.

"Hey! Where've you been, Ellis?" Mum asks as I hurriedly clamber out. "I mean, I saw your note, but I thought you were just somewhere in the grounds. And when I came out and couldn't see you I started to. . . Oh!"

Mum has just caught sight of Mr Fraser's other passenger. Perhaps, with the shine of the windscreen, she'd thought at first that it was Cam keeping me company. But as RJ's daughter swings herself and her rucksack out of the van, hair fluttering and flopping around her shoulders, it's pretty obvious that it's someone very different.

"Eloise?" Mum says hesitantly.

Whoa. Does she recognize RJ's daughter from photos he's shown her? Or is it just the fact that Eloise looks – now I have a second to secretly study the girl properly – really, really like him?

"Hello," Eloise says to Mum, with sub-zero warmth in her voice. "I thought my dad was going to be here. When will he be back?"

Eloise's red hair is flapping in the wind like a banner. She is as rangy and tall as her father and she towers over my tiny mum. But while RJ only ever looks at Mum with total, obvious, sometimes slightly *embarrassing* adoration, Eloise is gazing at my mother with something that's hovering between indifference and dislike.

(Out of the corner of my eye, I suddenly see another fleeting glimmer of light coming from the garden, same as I did this morning. When I have time, and the world isn't so weird, I might have to go and see what shiny something is lurking out there.)

"Your dad isn't going to be here for quite a while, Eloise. Listen, come on inside and we can talk," Mum says to her, before turning, as an afterthought, to our builder.

"Sorry – are you OK to get on with what you need to do, Mr Fraser?" she checks with him, while he clatters and clanks tools out of the back of his van.

"Call me Gordon. And yes, Mrs Johnstone, I'll be fine."

Eloise has her back to me, but I see her positively shudder at the way Mr Fraser's just addressed Mum. I suppose *her* mother was Mrs Johnstone, once upon a time. Beth Johnstone. I know that because I read it in *Heat* in the café yesterday when Mum was looking aghast at the photos. . .

"And call me Sadie, please," Mum replies, almost

to Eloise as much as Mr Fraser. With that, she ushers Eloise inside.

I go to follow – but it seems like I'm not allowed to. Mum's put her hand lightly on my arm, as a stop signal.

"Ellis, once we're upstairs, can you just give me and Eloise a bit of time on our own?"

Mum is looking at me pleadingly.

I don't want Mum to keep secrets from me. Secrets that she seems happily able to share with this complete stranger with the backpack.

"Sure, fine, whatever," I say sulkily. Barging past Mum, I head inside. Eloise is already on the stairs, and turns to look down on me. But she needn't worry – I'm not going to inflict my company on her. Instead, I turn and push open the heavy door that will lead me through to the passage by the old kitchen. I'm not sure where I'm going, but I'd rather be here in the cool, silent, empty warren of rooms than upstairs, hearing the vague murmur of conversation I'm not allowed to be part of.

Ding-a-ling!

I stop and look up at the wall here in the passage, and see something I hadn't noticed before: a whole board of polished bells on coils of brass.

Ding-a-ling!

The bells are so beautiful, and – like the old blackened range in the kitchen – one of the few original features of the house not to have been sold off, scavenged or stolen over the decades, I guess. Moving closer, I gaze up at the board, so I can read the lettering under each bell.

I haven't spotted any remaining bell pulls or buzzers in the rooms so far, so I'm guessing what's ringing is the front-door bell. Mr Fraser is probably armed with his electric screwdriver and fixing something out there, ahead of the other tradesmen Mum has coming in the next few days.

Ding-a-ling! the bell goes more frantically.

As I peer at the perfectly painted copperplate lettering, my fingertips press against the cold wall – and begin to tingle.

Words … words are tickling and crackling and wending their way from the dry touch of the plaster, through my hands, my arms, and up into my mind.

"*Where is she? Where is she?*" the voice hisses.

A metallic clattering rattles into my hearing too. Alarmed, I whip my fingers off the walls, just as the bell *ding-a-lings* again even more frantically.

Nursery says the sign below it.

I jump as a girl barges through the door I used just a second ago. In both hands she's clutching large empty tin jugs, which make it impossible for her to brush back the damp curls from round her face. It's the servant girl, the one who'd had the horrid, spoilt little boy upstairs try and get her into trouble.

So I *wasn't* imagining what happened earlier.

Or maybe I'm just going even more insane that ever...

"Flora! FLORA! Is that you, girl?" a woman's voice bellows from the kitchen. "Get yourself in here this moment."

I hold my breath, and hold myself steady, still, willing Flora not to see me.

But from her pinched white face and with stress pinking her cheeks, I can tell that all she's focusing on is the woman yelling for her. Right now, I'm as visible as the steam I feel wisping from the kitchen doorway right next to me.

"Yes, Mrs Strachan!" I hear Flora say as she scurries into the busy, noisy room.

"Where on earth have you *been*?!" the scary voice roars. "Jean's looking for you. Miss Matilda requested bathwater for Master Archibald half an hour ago, so he can be ready for the photographer that's coming. She and Catriona have been waiting in the nursery all this time for you to bring it."

All these names ... names of people who look real, or sound real, but *can't* be real. Still, in this moment, they seem as alive and in the here and now as I am. Though I'm not alive to them, am I?

I'm more like ... like a *ghost* from the future, who's turned a corner in time and become an unseen eavesdropper to the past.

But even in my strange, invisible state, I don't dare stroll right on into the kitchen and nosy at whatever drama is unfolding. Instead, I opt for inching along the wall, and peeking in the crack between the open door and its frame.

From my limited viewpoint, I can see a large, imposing middle-aged woman glowering at Flora. This Mrs Strachan has an impressive bunch of keys hanging from a chain around her waist, which makes me think she's the housekeeper here at Wilderwood.

A girl paler and scrawnier than Flora is lifting a heavy copper pan from the huge range, using cloths and surprising strength. Another woman, small, chubby and with rosy cheeks, is thunking dough on a long table, puffs of flour exploding as high as her elbows with every blow.

"I'm sorry, I – I—" Flora begins to stammer apologetically as she takes the copper pan from the other girl and hurriedly begins to pour it into her waiting jugs.

"Never mind your sorries, madam. Minnie practically boiled this water away waiting for you," the housekeeper roars on. "Don't you know Mrs Wallace has need for the stove, without these bath kettles cluttering the place up?"

"I didn't mean to—"

"Yes, you never mean to do anything, do you, Flora Dean? And yet—"

"Oww!" comes a screech. "Mrs Strachan – Flora just scalded me!"

I didn't quite see what happened there; only that the girl Minnie (the kitchen maid?) is clutching her damp foot, trying to pull the wool of her black stocking off her skin to cool it.

"It was an accident, Minnie!" Flora insists desperately. "I'm sorry. I—"

"Out – out of here NOW, Flora..."

At the latest roar from the fearsome housekeeper, I leap back, out of sight, just as Flora comes running empty-handed out of the kitchen, her white apron held over her face as she sobs.

She hurries back the way she came, the heavy door slamming shut behind her.

Something makes me want to follow.

Passing the kitchen doorway, I risk a quick glance in. I see that the room is bare of noise, rush, clutter, and of life. The strangeness of this other world is gone, and I feel – I feel empty. Still, I yank open the heavy door and look up the stone stairs, wistfully wishing I could see a flurry of black skirts and boots.

But Flora isn't here. Or is it that I'm not *there*?

Clunk!

I jerk at the sound of the back door clicking shut. Flora? Or is it Mr Fraser? The trouble is, I have no idea ... not *where* but *when* I am exactly. Maybe I'll find out, if I follow whoever went outdoors just now. My heart thunders as I put my hand on the big brass knob and twist it open.

A cool wind hits me.

Stepping into the fresh air, I wonder for a moment which way to go, but it's as if the breeze is blowing me down the short side of the East Wing, towards the front of the house.

Or maybe the breeze isn't to blame. Perhaps it's the sound of sobbing that draws me on. Or the burbling of water in the beautiful, ivy-free fountain. Flora is perched on the granite lip of it, her face still covered by her apron.

As I draw closer to her, shock hits me. I'm shocked to realize that I don't feel frightened. I have no idea why that is. All I know is that it doesn't matter whether whiplash or hunger or even anaemia is causing my mind to play these wonderful, startling tricks on me. What does matter is that right at this second, there are no waves rolling in; I don't feel a single ripple of anxiety.

With only curiosity and calmness inside me, I walk towards the girl, my feet making no noise on the newly laid paving stones.

Then I watch, fascinated, as Flora slowly, warily drops her hands from her face. She raises her head and gazes off towards the grand, ornate, and probably locked gates at the bottom of the driveway. I wonder if she's focusing on the road beyond them that leads to the village ... perhaps wishing she could just walk through those gates and down that road and escape this place.

Now I can see the freckles across her nose and the

deep brown of her big, blinking eyes. More unruly curls than ever are escaping from her white cap.

I'm so busy staring and studying her, that it takes me completely by surprise when Flora turns her head sharply.

"Hello," she says, her brown eyes locked on mine.

The girl's words are like a slap to my face. This is different. Wildly, madly different. This really isn't some mirage in my mind. I'm looking directly into the eyes of a living, breathing girl from another time, another version of Wilderwood Hall – and she's looking directly back into mine.

"You can . . . you can see me?" I mumble, tripping over my words.

"Aye, but why is it that I can see you and others cannot?" says Flora.

Her chest is heaving, as if there's a bird locked and frightened inside of it, fluttering and trying to fly free.

"I don't know, but please don't be scared," I tell her, holding my hands up imploringly.

She clasps a hand to her chest and looks ready to run.

"Actually, right now, I'm a bit scared too," I add, hoping it makes her feel better.

My honesty makes her pause at least. She looks me up and down, her eyes widening, scandalized by my lack of skirt I'm sure. Wherever and whenever I am, to a girl like Flora, leggings must seem like I'm walking around next to naked.

"What are you?" she demands. "Some kind of selkie?"

"A selkie?" I say, wondering if it's some kind of Scottish slang for an English person. "What is that?"

"A beastie that once was a seal. That rises from the sea and takes on human form," Flora jabbers on, sounding panicked. "You *are* a selkie, I know it! My grandmother herself said she saw them when she was a girl growing up in Oban. She said she went down to the shore and played with them. No one ever believed her stories but me."

The girl's eyes are huge in her gaunt face, fear only a scream away, I worry. Oh, but she *mustn't* scream – or I'm likely to scream too, and I don't know *who* that might alert. The fierce housekeeper or someone else from this *older* Wilderwood? The possibility of that makes me deeply uneasy.

"I'm not a ... a seal or a selkie," I tell Flora quickly. "I'm just a normal girl."

"I think you are *not*, miss," she announces. "You – you may seem it now, as you are, but earlier you were the strangest thing to me. A haze that became a figure and then faded to nothing. You appeared and were gone so quickly that I could not trust my own eyes!"

And now I know for sure: I didn't just imagine being on the beautifully furnished first-floor landing this morning, any more than I imagined the noise and steam and clatter of the busy kitchen a few minutes ago. And I'm definitely not imagining the terrified girl standing staring only inches away from me.

"So you did see me this morning?" I ask her. "When you were hiding in that room, or store cupboard, or whatever it is..."

"In my closet, you mean?" asks Flora.

"Your closet?" I repeat, wishing I knew more about whatever era I've slipped into. Perhaps "closet" meant something different to a cupboard back then. "Do you . . . *live* in there?"

Flora suddenly does something I don't expect, and I don't suppose she does either.

She bursts out laughing.

But just as quickly, she reigns in the smiles and glances around alarmed at the French doors at the front of the house. Flora's worried, I suppose, that she might be discovered. I don't suppose the wealthy family who own the house would want their staff enjoying the fountain or any other part of the estate that wasn't strictly the servants' domain.

"Of course not!" she says, answering my question now in a voice not much louder than a whisper. "The closet is where I keep the coal for the fires and empty the chamber pots."

Flora wrinkles her nose as she speaks.

"You're a maid," I state, more for my own sake than hers. I'm sure Flora is all too certain of her role.

"My name is Flora," she informs me, though she's still sounding wary. "I am the under-housemaid here at Wilderwood."

"My name is Ellis," I tell her in reply. "I live here now."

Flora's face drops and her mouth hangs open. My truth is too far-fetched for her.

"You do not!" snaps Flora, taken aback by my clearly false statement. "You are no guest of the master and mistress. *I* would know."

Flora *would* know, I suppose, because she'd be cleaning out my chamber pot, if that was the case.

"Oh, but I don't live in the main house," I begin to *try* to explain, knowing it's going to be difficult, if not impossible, since I have no words to explain to *myself* what's happening. "I mean, me and my mother, we're staying up *there*," I say, pointing to the first floor of the East Wing.

"No, no!" Flora answers back, shaking her head fervently, which frees more curls. "That is the servants' quarters. Only Mrs Strachan has her rooms there, along with Miss Matilda and Jean and Ann and Minnie and me."

All these names ... who are these women and girls? I only recognize the governess's name. And back in the kitchen there was mention of Mrs Wallace (the cook? The small, round woman bashing the bread dough?) and someone called Catriona. Where do *they* sleep, I wonder? And what about the male servants that I saw in the photo in the café?

In the crazed whirl of confusion and questions crowding my mind, something suddenly occurs to me, and I have an instant, burning desire to know the answer to one particular question.

"Which room is yours?" I ask, wondering, hoping against hope that it's the same as mine. Somehow that might make some strange kind of sense of all this.

"You see the one closest? With the gable?" says Flora.

Yes, yes, it IS mine! I think to myself.

"It's across the hall from there. I bunk up with Minnie."

Oh ... so Flora sleeps – or at least once slept – in the cobweb-curtained room where our futon is currently dumped, I realize with disappointment. Hey, maybe I love coincidences as much as Mum does, and *that's* why me and Flora "sharing" a room seemed to matter for a second there.

Hold on. . .

As Mum flutters into my consciousness, I feel the familiar ripple and roll of anxiety. Me being here, properly here with Flora, talking to her ... what does that mean? I'm not here for good, am I? I can go back to my time – can't I?

"Wait!" Flora bursts into my panicked thoughts. "Are *you* the shadow that comes in my sleep?"

"What?" I reply, lost with her mentions of selkies and shadows, as well as my own sudden worries.

"I have been having the strangest dreams," Flora carries on, her voice getting louder as her excitement builds. "I turn a corner and see a glimpse of a shadow . . . and then it is gone. Is that you?"

"Me? No!" I say, shaking my head.

All of a sudden, I feel a sharp longing for Mum, now that everything is becoming more unsettling and bizarre.

"Wait! I know it now," gasps Flora, her thin hand at her mouth in shock. "In her village, the people said my grandmother was a seer . . . I must be like her! I have had the dreams, and now here you are like an apparition before me. I have inherited her talent, have I not?"

A seer. That's like a wise woman, isn't it? Someone with supernatural powers. . .

Oh, please, please let me get back to Mum, I wordlessly plead, as shivers get the better of me.

And as I picture Mum's sweet smile and the pink tips of her blonde hair, I feel something. A kind of tug at my back. As if someone is yanking at my jumper, trying to get my attention.

"Oh, we'd better go – quick!" I hear Flora say urgently, and see her leap from the fountain's edge at the sound of a rattle and clank. She holds out her hand to me, but in the space of time between me looking towards the source of the noise – one of the French doors being pushed open on to the terrace – and back again, Flora is gone. And so is the tugging sensation.

Where Flora stood, there's nothing but a leftover autumn leaf blowing by in the spring winds. It lands not on water, but in the tangle of ivy that covers and smothers the fountain.

Relief runs warm through my veins. I can dip in to Flora's world and come safely back to mine. It makes me want to find her quickly, to make sure she's OK and not in any trouble...

"All right?" Mr Fraser interrupts my thoughts, as he steps out on to the moss-covered terrace and spots me standing stock-still and open-mouthed. I must look like someone who's trying to remember where they've left their mind.

"Mmm," I mumble uselessly, then turn to go, aiming myself away from the builder and towards the back door.

Unfortunately, I also aim myself directly into Cam, stepping on *both* his feet.

"Oof!" he gasps. The two sheepdogs at his side start barking excitedly, like it's some kind of game.

It's not a game, and it was just an accident. A normal reaction would be to say sorry and move on. But I've had plenty of experience of boys (and girls) braying at me at my old school, where saying sorry just got drowned out in all the cruel laughter and teasing.

And apart from that, life doesn't feel very normal right now. So "sorry" is not what I come out with. Nowhere near.

"Why are you here again?" I snap at Cam, sounding a lot angrier than I mean to.

Cam looks at me with his scanning blackbird eyes, as if he's trying to work out what my problem is, or squirrel his way into my thoughts or something. Bet he's loving this; some giraffe-sized, gangly girl making a fool of herself in front of him, for the second time today.

"Dad texted me to say he forgot this," Cam says calmly, holding up a tool that I think might be a widget or a wrench or very possibly *neither* of these things because I don't know what I'm talking about and I'm *beside* myself with embarrassment.

"Oh, OK. Fine, then," I answer stupidly, flicking my hand away from a nosy dog's tongue that's just licked there.

Then just as I try to hang on to the faintest scrap of dignity and move away, I see one of those tiny split-second twinkles of light in the corner of my eye. Cam turns in the direction of it – he must've spotted it too.

"What was that?" he asks, frowning in the direction of the bushes down by the open entrance to Wilderwood.

I don't know if the sparkles of light I've seen today have anything to do with Flora and what's been happening to me, but I know that it's none of this stranger's business.

"What was what? I didn't see anything," I snipped at Cam, then stomp off to see what's happening inside the house with Mum, with Eloise, or very possibly the past...

Wandering this way and that, drifting from room to room. . .

For quite a while I searched the main house for Flora, hoping I might touch some tattered piece of wallpaper and hear a whisper to guide me to her. Hoping I might turn some random corner and stumble across her hurrying about her duties. But perhaps Mr Fraser's banging and crashing in *this* Wilderwood stopped me tuning in to the other, older version of the Hall.

Finally I gave up on finding Flora and headed here, to the servants' quarters, keeping my fingers crossed that Mum and Eloise will be done with their cosy, private little chat. But they're not.

Hovering outside Mum's office, I hold my breath, trying to catch some of the conversation.

Not that I'm used to it, but I can't hear Eloise's voice; only Mum's. *Her* voice is saying stilted "yes, but"s and "no, but"s mostly, with long silences in between. She must be on the phone. Talking to RJ? I don't think so . . . Mum would sound happier, surely.

"Look, her dad will want her back at school too, but—"

Mum is silent again, as the person at the other end interrupts.

I wonder what this is about; won't Eloise be off for the holidays anyway? Or do private schools and boarding schools have different term times from regular ones?

"Yes, Beth, but—"

Mum just called the other person "Beth". Of course; that's the name of RJ's ex-wife, Eloise's mum. Is she flipping out? Didn't she know that Eloise was planning to come here? Maybe she thought Eloise was hard at work at her fancy boarding school in wherever, and not travelling up the west coast of the country on a train bound for Scotland. . .

The sudden creak of a chair from inside makes me leap away from the door as if it had turned burning hot. The last thing I want to do is be caught eavesdropping, either by Mum or, especially, by Eloise. I'm not exactly keen to face that dead-eyed glower. And so I hurry into my own room, pushing the door shut as silently as I can behind me.

Letting out a long, slow breath, I walk over to the two windows of my bedroom and gaze out across the grounds and treetops, towards the village in the distance. I'm facing east, of course, but right now my heart yearns for the south. For faraway London. For a friendly voice from home.

Pulling my phone out of my back pocket, I press Shaniya's number on the screen, and hope she'll pick up.

"Come on, come on, come on. . ." I mutter as the dialling tone burrs.

"Hey, Ellis!" she says, sounding brighter than she did earlier. Good.

"Hi. Listen, is now OK to talk?" I check with her.

"Ha! You sound like a spy, about to tell me some secret of national importance!"

There she goes, slipping into the joking straight away. But I'm not sure I'm in a joking mood. Everything about today so far is too overwhelming, too deeply strange to joke about.

"Look, I just wanted to tell you what's been going on," I begin, hoping Shaniya can hear the urgency in my voice and know I'm not fooling around. "Things have got pretty crazy around here."

"What – been hearing more ghostly voices? MWAH HA HA!"

I go instantly cold. Not because of Shaniya's fake evil laugh but because of the other voices I can hear laughing now.

"Who's there?" I ask her.

"I'm just with the girls. We're going to hang out at Camden Market this afternoon. Oh, here comes the bus. Talk to you later, yeah?"

With a dull, soft click my connection to London is gone.

Putting the phone down on to the windowsill, I begin to idly twirl it around on the dusty surface, all the while wishing, wishing, wishing. . .

With Shaniya too busy with our other friends to miss me, I wish there was someone, anyone else I could call right now and tell them about my insane Day Two at Wilderwood Hall. Like a grandparent. I mean, I wish I had the sort of granny who wouldn't mind me calling her at strange times of the day, not if I really needed a chat. The sort who likes to hear you yak about dumb stuff like how cute your new trainers are and doesn't just grill you about your latest marks in school tests.

And sometimes I wish I had a dad I could phone once in a while, who cared about me even if he lived thousands of miles away. Well, part of that is true; my dad *does* live thousands of miles away, in Florida, with his pretty wife and three adorable little kids, who he loves madly, it looks like from his Facebook profile. I sneak a peek at it from time to time.

I'm still wishing and twirling when I suddenly remember something. The photo I took in the café this morning, of the print on the wall.

Quickly, I find it and click – there it is. Flick, flick, *flick* and it's as enlarged as I can make it on my small screen.

Flitting from one face to the other, I study the faces I don't know: Mr and Mrs Richards, *lots* of male servants, three maids I haven't glimpsed in my fleeting visits to the other, long-ago Wilderwood yet. Are these . . . I try to remember the names Flora mentioned . . . Jean, Ann and Catriona?

Then there are the faces I've *definitely* seen: Mrs Strachan the housekeeper, Mrs Wallace the cook,

Miss Matilda the governess, Minnie the kitchen maid, and Flora, of course.

Everyone in the image – from top-hatted Mr Richards to the lowliest servant – holds themselves stern and steady and somewhat proudly. Everyone except for the fidgety little boy, of course. And Flora. She is staring directly into the camera lens, chin dropped defensively towards her chest, her expression weary and worn, like a badly treated dog waiting for its next beating.

Poor Flora ... if I could see her, comfort her, somehow reach out (reach *back*?) and help her.

Then a thought pops sharply into my head: down in the old kitchens, Flora was being told off for not having the water ready for the little boy's bath. And Mrs Strachan said Archibald must be ready for the photographer coming. For *this* actual photograph. . . ? It had to be! A professional photographer coming to your house in those days would have been a very big deal, so—

"Ellis? Ellis?"

I move so fast when I hear Mum shouting for me that I nearly drop my phone as I try and stuff it back in my pocket.

"Hi!" I say, stumbling out into the corridor.

Mum quickly slaps on a smile when she sees me, though she looks exhausted. She seems tinier than ever, as if all her energy has been sucked out of her. Eloise is close behind, mouth tight and eyes fixed to the ground. But straight away I can tell that she's been crying; her eyes are red-rimmed behind her cool geek glasses. It's not as if I know her well enough to go give her a hug, but it's actually not the fact that my brand-new stepsister is a stranger that stops me. Eloise just doesn't seem to be the sort of person who'd appreciate an arm around her shoulder. She prickles with some kind of leave-me-alone emotional electrical fence.

"Right, then!" Mum says, all brittle with fake brightness. "Eloise—"

"Wheezy," Eloise says bluntly.

For a second, I'm confused. Is she telling us she feels ill? Is she asthmatic, maybe?

"Oh, yes . . . sorry. Ellis, Eloise likes to be known by her nickname," Mum explains to me. "So *Weezy*, I'll get you a towel, and you can have a shower. We've got lots of nice gel and shampoo and things in the bathroom, so help yourself."

"Weezy" barely acknowledges what Mum has just said.

"And meanwhile, Ellis, we can fix up the futon and make that room opposite yours a bit more comfortable for Weezy. Right?"

Now it's *my* turn to barely acknowledge Mum. This Weezy girl is *staying*? How long for?! RJ isn't due back for another month. She can't stay here all that time, can she? *Can* she? Doesn't she need to be back at her school, or home with her mum or something?

"Sure," I finally reply, and go to grab the blue IKEA bag of spare bedding that's been sitting in the corridor with all the other still-to-be-put-away boxes and bags. My head reeling, I lug it off towards the "guest" bedroom, and dump the bulging bag on the floor next to the folded-up futon. Even though it's on the first floor, this room is dark and dingy, and extra cold too, I think, gazing around.

I should put the light on, I decide, and walk over to flip the ancient-looking round switch. I'll probably get electrocuted, knowing my luck. . .

But oh . . . it's not *pain* I feel flickering in my finger. The prickles turn to tap-tap-tapping, as if a message is being telegraphed to me, travelling up the length of my arm.

"Guh-guh-guh. . ."

The taps turn to a soft sound. I press my fingers

harder on the chipped white ceramic switch, the better to "listen".

"*Guh-guh-GUH!*" the sound continues, growing steadily louder, as a word begins to form.

And then I leap out of my skin as a tall blonde girl rushes past me and into the room.

"GET DOWNSTAIRS RIGHT NOW!" she shrieks at someone.

I whip around and see the room as dark and dingy as ever, but with a thin curtain at the window and not just cobwebs. Two sagging beds are pressed up against each wall, an unsteady small table between them with a stub of candle in a tin holder resting on it. On one wall is a single framed picture of a posy of mauve pansies. It tries and fails to cheer the room.

Of course, this is where Flora sleeps. But where is she?

The shrieking girl, dressed in a housemaid's outfit same as Flora's, slams the door shut and exposes Flora, who is standing (hiding?) behind it.

"I came to pin my hair, Jean," Flora mumbles, pointing at the small, chipped mirror on the wall. "Mrs Strachan told me that I was to tidy myself up, before the photographer gentleman summons us."

Flora has metal pins between her teeth, I see. She's trying to fix her unruly, springy curls before they get her into more trouble.

"You've had PLENTY of time to do that!" the young woman called Jean yells.

"But on the way here Catriona saw me and asked that I stoke the nursery fire while she got afternoon tea for the young master and Miss Matilda!" Flora says, her bottom lip trembling.

"Excuses! You *always* have excuses, don't you, Flora? Well, I'll be having a word with Mrs Strachan about this and see about docking your wages for—"

I can't bear it any more. All I've heard are people nipping and niggling and sniping at Flora today. How can she stand to be treated in this way? How can she put up with a life like this? I can't *bear* bullying. The idea that someone can have such power over you, that they can make a fool of you and talk to you like you're dirt. . .

So without thinking it through, or even thinking if it's *possible*, I do something. I reach over and tug at the bow of Jean's apron.

"What?" she shrieks as it flaps loose and falls to the floor. Flora's hands fly to her mouth to stop a laugh spurting out.

"Just – just get yourself downstairs," mutters Jean, bending quickly to gather up her apron and bustling out of the room.

It's then that Flora lets her hands fall from her face and looks at me.

"How is it that you could do that?" she asks. "What kind of spirit are you?"

My heart starts pounding. I don't know how it is that I'm suddenly able to do a physical action in this other Wilderwood. I thought I was just an observer, as visible in this world as air, to everyone but Flora.

"I'm not a spirit," I say quickly. "I'm just a normal person. And I live . . . in another time, and another way, in this house."

I hope that's enough of an explanation for her. . . I recognize that Flora is a frightened, bullied girl, and I don't want to frighten her any more by claiming to be from some freaky future plane.

But Flora needs more.

"*What* other time?" she demands.

"Tell me this year first," I ask, stalling as I try and get my thoughts straight.

"Why, it's 1912. April, 1912," Flora answers, her brown eyes locked on mine, waiting for my reply.

"OK . . . well, I live here more than a century later. It's April too, but April 2016."

"April 2016," Flora repeats, her eyes dark and her skin pale with shock. "When I am long, long dead."

"And I'm not even born in your world," I add, not wanting her to dwell on that last fact. "I'm not alive for another ninety-one years."

We both stare at each other, eyebrows raised, absorbing these head-twisting truths.

"I don't understand," Flora says at last, her face a picture of bewilderment.

"Neither do I," I say with a shrug.

"Can you come and go from here to . . . to *there* whenever you want?" asks Flora, stepping a little closer to me, her eyes frantically scanning, taking in every detail of me.

"I don't know how this works. This morning, when you saw me on the landing by the nursery, it was the first time it's ever happened."

"Oh, how my grandmother would have loved this!" Flora says in an excited whisper, now gently touching me on the cheek to confirm to herself that I'm a living, breathing girl. A ripple of pity hits me as I feel the roughness of her calloused hands. "If only I could tell her I have her gift. . ."

"Your gran; she's not alive any more?" I ask.

"No. She passed just after my parents sent me here to work," says Flora.

It suddenly occurs to me that Flora doesn't look much older than me.

"How old are you?" I ask her.

"Fourteen last birthday. Same as Minnie. . ."

Flora looks over at one of the beds in the room with a bitter expression.

"Minnie is the kitchen maid; is that right?" I say, remembering the girl's accusation that Flora had deliberately spilt boiling water on her.

"And Cook's pet," Flora replies. "Same as Jean the head housemaid is Mrs Strachan's pet, and Catriona the nursery maid is Miss Matilda's pet, and Ann the ladies' maid is the mistress's pet. Everyone here is someone's pet – everyone except for *me*. . ."

Flora looks suddenly so forlorn, so lonely, that I reach out to touch her arm, but then everything changes back. Or is that forward? Because Mum has just charged in between us with a table lamp in her hand and a colourful throw over her shoulder.

"Sorry, sorry, sorry, sweetheart!" she says,

dumping the lamp and rug down and gathering me up in a sudden hug. "I know that it's a bit of a shock having Eloise – I mean *Weezy* – turn up out of the blue like this."

I glance over Mum's shoulder and see that Flora is gone, that there is nothing on the wall but a faint oval patch on the faded paintwork where a mirror might have once hung.

"What's going on?" I ask Mum, hoping I seem normal, and not part-lost in the other Wilderwood. "Why's Elo— Weezy here?"

"She ran away. OK, maybe she didn't quite *run away* exactly – she has just turned eighteen, after all," Mum qualifies, "but let's say she left home on the spur of the moment to come find RJ, and confront him."

"Confront him about what?"

"Look, it's all a bit of a disaster," Mum says, lowering her voice, although I can now clearly hear the rush and the gurgle of water from the shower room down the corridor.

"A disaster how?" I ask, watching Mum bite the inside of her lip.

"It turns out that Weezy didn't know anything about the wedding. . ."

"*Your* wedding?" I ask Mum dumbly, as I try and get my focus back to the here and now.

"Yes," she says, dropping her arms from around me and peering warily in the direction of the corridor, as if she's worried that Weezy will appear in the doorway in nothing but a towel and an accusing stare. "She found out about it on Twitter."

Wow. My first impressions of Weezy might not be good, but even *I* can see how harsh it would be to find out your dad had remarried via social media.

"RJ didn't tell her?" I say, shocked. He'd dropped her into conversation quite a lot, and sounded like a loving, mad-for-his-girl dad to me. I feel a tiny shiver of panic. How well does Mum really know RJ? How can we have deleted our whole old life for him and Wilderwood Hall, if he's like some kind of heartless wolf in disguise?

"RJ tried, but it turns out Weezy had changed her number and her email address without telling him," says Mum, blinking up at me with blue eyes framed with wings of black eyeliner. "She quit Facebook too, so he couldn't contact her that way. And of course he tried to contact her via Beth, Weezy's mum, but those messages didn't get through."

"She didn't pass them on?" I ask.

"Didn't pass the messages on, or his letters, *or* the wedding invitation. Well, she *said* she did, and that Weezy didn't want to go."

"That's seriously bad," I mumble.

Either Weezy's mum is one bitter ex-wife, or – and I can't say this to Mum – RJ is one bad ex-husband and dad, which is why Beth acted that way...

"So, understandably, Weezy is furious with her mum for hiding the invitation and various letters and furious with her father for not trying harder to get in touch with her directly. Though I'm not exactly sure what else he was meant to do."

"Go visit her at her school and see her face-to-face?" I suggest.

"That's another disaster; Weezy dropped out of her school a few weeks ago," says Mum, ruffling her blonde hair with her hands. "And her A levels are coming up soon. Oh, I wish RJ was here! It's too hard trying to sort this out when he's constantly on the move and we can't get a reliable connection either end..."

"Was this why you were on the phone this morning?" I ask, remembering Mum's unexpected irritation with me.

"Yes – RJ was trying to fill me in on everything before he got on a plane."

"But why didn't you just tell me what was happening?" I frown at her.

"Ellis, you weren't well yesterday, on top of having to contend with this big move and the huge change. I didn't want to overload you with stuff to worry about," says Mum, gently rubbing my arm.

"What – and I wouldn't find about it when Weezy showed up here?" I say.

"Babes, we didn't know that's what was going to happen," Mum says apologetically. "This morning her mum called RJ to say Weezy and her clothes and rucksack and stuff had gone sometime overnight. They didn't know if she'd just taken off to stay with a friend, or maybe even seen sense and gone back to her boarding school. To be honest, I was hoping to hear that Weezy had called her mum and was fine, so that you wouldn't have had to know or stress about anything."

"But here she is," I say, feeling a ripple of worry in my chest.

"Yes, here she is," Mum says with a shrug. "Turns out she came across all the letters her Mum had hidden, including the one where her dad told her about buying this place. So . . . *ta-da!*"

Mum holds out her hands, a wry, what-can-we-do? limp smile on her face. But I can't smile back.

I don't want to be in the middle of some other family's feud right now, as well as everything else.

(The waves start rolling. . .)

"Hey, are you OK, Ellis?" Mum asks, frowning at me. "You're looking a bit pale all of a sudden. Is all of this too much?"

"I'm fine," I lie, though I feel a flicker of pleasure at having her full attention for the first time in hours today. "Haven't eaten much today, so maybe it's that."

"Oh, Ellis . . . what am I thinking? We need to get some food into you," says Mum, snapping into action. "Let's leave setting up this room till later. I'll get some pasta on for you now and maybe some—"

Mum's phone trills from the pocket of her jeans and she grabs it out super fast.

"RJ!" Mum says, her face breaking into a smile of relief. "RJ – can you hear me? You're cutting out. . . Sorry, Ellis – I have to take this."

And so, after Mum gives me her undivided attention for all of two minutes, she leaves me again, hurrying off down the corridor and shutting the door of her own bedroom firmly behind her. What is going on with her today? Since when does she have to leave me to have a conversation with RJ? Specially when she's just told me everything.

Unless ... unless she *hasn't* quite told me everything.

'Cause I suddenly have a niggling feeling that Mum's keeping something back, keeping something secret from me right now.

But hey, *I've* got a pretty strange and special secret of my *own*. And if Mum isn't willing to let me in on hers, then I think I'll keep mine to myself too...

"Now wait till you see this!" says Mum, with all the over-the-top enthusiasm of a kids' TV presenter.

You can't blame her. She finally prised Weezy out of the spare room and said that we'd give her a guided tour of Wilderwood. Weezy grudgingly came, but looked about as pleased as if we'd offered to give her a Chinese burn. So far the three of us have trudged around the whole scuzzy house: Mum smiling, Weezy scowling and me trailing behind silent and stressed.

We've now come out of the back door by the kitchens and crossed the moss-covered yard where Mr Fraser's van is parked. We're standing in front of the boarded-tight stable block, and my tiny mum is tugging at one of the large pair of wooden doors that don't seem too keen on opening.

"This is the part of the Shiny New Plan that your dad is most looking forward to!" Mum says breathlessly, as she yanks hard at the non-budging, iron door handle.

"'Shiny New Plan'?" Weezy repeats, wrinkling her nose as if a bad smell had just wafted by.

"Well, our joint *project*, then," Mum says, pinking up around the cheeks with both effort and irritation, I think. Looks like Weezy is determined not to make any of this easy.

"Do you want me to give it a try?" I ask Mum, pointing to the door.

"Go on, then." Mum gives in and steps aside. "Mr Fraser had it open earlier, but he did say the wood is swollen and damp."

As I grab the handle – rust flaking and crackling under my fingers – I see Weezy gaze off at the gardens, nibbling at her nails. I wonder what she's thinking. That she can't bear to stay here more than one night, hopefully, especially since her dad isn't around and isn't due back for weeks. . .

"So anyway, Weezy, RJ is going to turn this building into a state-of-the-art recording studio," Mum tries to continue, with more forced cheerfulness. "And though the space needs to be opened up, he's planning to keep some of the original . . . horse areas or whatever you call them."

"Stalls," Weezy corrects her.

I'm still struggling with the reluctant door, but I manage a quick peek in Weezy's direction and see that she might be talking to Mum but she's not so much as glanced her way.

"Stalls, of course! Silly me," says Mum. "Have you done much riding, Weezy?"

Hearing Mum ask that almost makes me snigger. It sounds like the sort of thing a country landowner might ask, not a city girl like Mum. Mind you, I suppose she *is* a country landowner now. . .

"A bit," Weezy replies, tugging the sleeves of her black hoodie down to cover her hands.

"Didn't your dad say that you have a riding stable near your school that you all have access to?"

"Yep."

"Oh, that must be nice. Your school sounds pretty impressive from the way RJ described it," says Mum, sounding as if she's struggling as much with the one-sided conversation as I am with the stiff door. Only I'm not struggling any more; with a quick thud of my shoulder against the dark-green, faded boards, the door finally gives in and yawns open.

That got Weezy's attention. Her head flips back round to face us just as Mum yelps, "High five, Ellis!" and holds up her hand to be slapped.

For a split second I see a hint of curiosity on Weezy's face, but it's instantly replaced with a dark scowl when she spots what's on the inside of Mum's wrist.

"What's wrong, Weezy?" asks Mum, letting her hand flop down as the mood shifts from fine to bleak.

"Why do you have this?" Weezy demands, reaching out for Mum's hand and roughly turning it over so the tattoo of the dainty white star is visible.

"I – I got it to match the one your dad has on *his* wrist. I thought it was beautiful." Mum stumbles over her words, looking up warily as Weezy looms over her. She's clearly wondering what's going on, same as I am.

"It is!" Weezy bursts out.

With that, she drops Mum's hand and storms off across the yard and towards the side of the house.

"I'd better go after her. . ." Mum mutters without a backward glance my way.

As Mum catches up with my so-called stepsister by the ivy-covered fountain, two things happen, in practically the same instant.

Far beyond Mum and Weezy, down by the bushes and the perimeter wall, I see another glimmer of light, that small sparkle that is clearly there one second and then just as quickly gone.

At the same time, a sound begins to vibrate softly in the palm of the hand that's wrapped around the iron handle. Up it weaves, prickling around my arm as I try to tune in to the whispering. Only this time it's not soft words that I'm hearing. It's a whinny.

That unexpected sound pushes the glimmer to the back of my mind. I spin myself around, still holding tight to the door handle ... which is now smooth and sleek with glossy black paint.

And a smell hits me: the warm, yeasty scent of fresh straw, and the spikier, harsher pong of manure.

I've gone back again, haven't I? I think, stepping gingerly inside the stable that's now alive with sound – more whinnying, the crunch of horses' teeth munching on hay, iron shoes clattering on cobbled stall floors. And there's one more sound. My name being called. . .

"Ellis? Is that you?"

I look directly up. There's a sort of mezzanine level, piled high with dry straw or hay. Flora bends out from the darkness of it and smiles at me.

"What are you doing up there?" I say softly, not sure who – apart from the horses – might hear us, but taking no chances.

"Taking a moment for myself before I'm shouted at to do the next task," she tells me. "Come up! The steps are just there. . ."

I hurry over and scramble up a rough-hewn ladder and join her. Gazing back down from here, I see four horses in their stalls, steam rising off their sleek coats. All four are staring up at us, probably hoping that we odd, two-legged creatures aren't about to eat their stores of feed.

"Want some?" says Flora, tearing apart a large, chunky slice of bread and butter and handing me a piece.

"Thanks," I say, suddenly realizing how hungry I am. I wasn't much in the mood for the bowl of pasta Mum made me after she'd finally finished her call with RJ – with all the strangeness of the day I had no appetite and only managed to half-heartedly eat a couple of mouthfuls of what tasted like soggy rubber.

"Mrs Wallace the cook leaves a few pieces of this in the kitchen for Jim the stable lad at this time of day," explains Flora. "But he is not a very nice sort. So I thought I might relieve him of one piece of his bread while no one was looking!"

Flora grins, but puts her hand over her mouth like a child caught doing something a little naughty. Is she waiting to see if I'm shocked? I look at how very skinny her arms are and can't help thinking that she must get pretty poor rations from the cook herself. So how could I begrudge her some extra food that no one will miss – except this Jim, of course.

"You seem happy," I tell her, wondering if there is something more making her smile than just a sneaked piece of bread and the peace of this stable hideaway. And then I remember the group portrait that must have happened by now. "Did you like having your photograph taken today?"

"How do you know that? Were you watching?" she asks in surprise.

"No – earlier, in your room, you told Jean that

Mrs Strachan had made you tidy your hair for the photographer coming."

"Ah, yes. But no, I did not like it," she says firmly. "Minnie accused me of pushing her on the steps where we were standing, so of course Cook gave me a clip around the ear for that."

"No wonder you pinched the bread, then," I say cheerfully, though my heart hurts for her.

"Oh, I am used to their mean ways," says Flora, with a bat of her hand. "But what of Minnie and Cook, when I have such news to tell you!"

I like to see her face so softened and sweet.

"What is it?" I ask, curious.

"I am to travel to America soon! Is that not something?"

Her brown eyes are soft with hope and excitement.

"To America?" I repeat with surprise.

In this long-ago time, a poorly paid housemaid like Flora would barely travel further than the local village on a rare day off, surely.

"It's the truth, I tell you!" she says, a smile lighting up her face. "When I was on the stairs just now, I heard Mr Stewart the butler talk of it to the governess. The whole household is to be packed up next week and we are to travel – *by train* – to the master's house in London. London! And from there we will go on to Southampton and then sail on a fine ocean liner all the way across the Atlantic, to New York. Can you imagine?"

"That sounds wonderful!" I say, genuinely excited for Flora. It's a trip *I* would be happy with, travelling first south, then away to somewhere so exciting, leaving drab, lonely Wilderwood behind. "I haven't been to New York, but London is amazing."

"You have visited it?" Flora asks in amazement.

"Until a few days ago, I lived there," I tell her.

"Oh, my! What is it like? Are there many fine buildings? Have you travelled on the Underground railway? Is it terribly fast?"

"Um, London is a very busy but interesting place," I begin, trying to answer all her quick-fire questions in order. "And yes, lots of the buildings are beautiful, but some areas are poorer, and the buildings aren't so grand. And yes, I've been on the Underground loads of times. It is fast, but it's just like being on a tram or a bus without the views."

This is fun. I thought talking about the future would frighten Flora. But so much of London is the same as it would have been in her time.

"And what of King George?" asks Flora. "Have you ever seen him?"

Of course ... certain places in London might have survived for a century or even more, but *people* wouldn't have.

"He's not around in my time," I say gently, trying to pick my words carefully so they're not too shocking. "I did stand outside Buckingham Palace on a school trip once, and we all thought we'd seen the queen at a window, but it probably wasn't her."

"The queen?" squeaks Flora, dropping her bread uneaten in her lap.

"Queen Elizabeth. The second Queen Elizabeth. I think your King George was maybe her grandfather?"

As I try in vain to remember anything I've learned or heard about British kings and queens, I feel Flora gather my hands in hers. As before, I'm guiltily aware of the rough, parched feel of her hard-working skin on my smooth fingers.

"Oh, Ellis," she says, smiling earnestly at me, "I still don't understand how it is that you can be here, but I feel that you have perhaps brought me luck! Because you *are* the shadow from my dreams, aren't you?"

"Look, I'd be very glad to think I've brought you luck, but I really don't feel I am some 'shadow'," I say, feeling confused, and a little uneasy again.

But perhaps I *have* been appearing to her, without being aware of it. If *I* can hear whisperings through time in the walls and floors of Wilderwood Hall, why isn't it possible that Flora would dream of me?

You know, maybe *I'm* some modern-day seer, without even knowing it. Maybe I inherited some second sight or something from a grandmother, same as Flora did!

Hey, it's a nice idea, but I doubt it. I've never met my dad's mum, of course, but my gran in Australia is about as psychic and spiritual as a paving stone.

The truth is, I don't know what anything means any more.

All I know is that with my everyday life feeling so tilted and strange right now, being with Flora is – bizarrely – the closest thing I have to normal.

"But do you not think it is wonderful that I dreamt of you, Ellis?" says Flora, her eyes wide and insistent. "*I* do. My friend from the future, my bringer of luck, twin of my heart. The two of us. . ."

I can see Flora's lips still moving as she finishes her sentence.

And now, after a moment's stillness and frowning, she's mouthing my name, urgently.

The thing is, I can't hear her. A soft vibration in my back pocket is growing louder, turning into a buzzing to that fills my ears and – and—

And Flora is gone.

I'm sitting perched alone on a bare, damp ledge of wobbly, rotten planks in the stable block.

There's no clatter and whinny of horses – just the ringing of my phone.

I grab it and am instantly glad of the warm, colourful glow of the screen in this dark, drab place.

And I'm even more glad to see that it's Shaniya calling me back!

This time, this time, I'll tell her everything and she'll listen and be amazed and tell me what I should do and what I should think because my head is upside down and inside out...

"Shaniya!"

"Hey! Sorry about earlier – I couldn't talk 'cause of the girls. You know how it is."

"That's all right," I say, with a pang of homesickness spearing my chest.

"So what's happening with you and Weirdwood

Hall, then? Any more freaky-deakiness I need to know about?"

"Today has been insane," I blurt out. "You'll never guess what just—"

"*Everything* in your life is insane at the moment, Ellis," Shaniya interrupts. "So go on; what's happening at the castle with the rock star stepdaddy?"

"What? It's – it's not a castle. It's just a big house. And RJ's not a 'star', he's just a musician."

"Yeah, a musician who's rich enough to buy a castle. Ha! And then there's *my* stepdad, the bus driver, who might buy me and my sister a Happy Meal from McDonald's this week if we're lucky..."

Now I'm sort of tripped up in my thinking. It happens sometimes with Shaniya. I'll be sure how I'm going to say something and then along she comes with the joking and I don't know where I am and have to restart my train of thought.

"RJ's daughter arrived here out of the blue this afternoon," I tell Shaniya, deciding to start with *that* piece of news first, before I hit her with the sledgehammer stuff about Flora.

"Yeah? Did she hear about the castle and want to come claim a wing of it for herself?"

Shaniya doesn't mean to sound blunt, it's just the way she is. But I wonder if I'm irritating her a bit.

You know, it's my fault if I am; I shouldn't try to explain all this stuff to her, not when she's in the wrong kind of mood. The thing is, Shaniya's great and good fun, but you have to time things right with her or conversations can feel as comfortable as paddling in a pond full of sharks.

"It's pretty bad. She's dropped out of her boarding school and then she ran out on her mum without telling her where she was going."

"Aw, the poor princess was having a hard time at her expensive boarding school, was she?"

Shaniya is yawning as she speaks.

I don't know whether what I'm saying is boring her or if it's just me in general.

"It's actually been kind of tough around here today," I try again, "'cause Eloise is either angry or not speaking, and Mum's being weird and I think there are things she's not telling me."

"What? Things like exactly how rich you all are now?" Shaniya swoops in with one of her boom-*tish* barbed comments.

My head is starting to pound. The thing is, I've

always been there for Shaniya, but the minute I try to talk to her about anything to do with *me* – my shyness, the awkwardness, riding the waves that roll – she brushes it off with jokes and banter. Jokes and banter that don't *always* come across as very funny or friendly. . .

"Listen, I know in some ways I seem lucky," I tell Shaniya now, while remembering how hard it's been for Mum bringing me up on her own all these years, how hard it is having a dad who deserted us, "but it's honestly not that great here."

I glance around at the wreck of a stable building, and think of the bigger wreck of Wilderwood, and feel suddenly very empty and far away and small inside.

"Aw . . . it'll be OK, Ellis," Shaniya drawls. "'Cause maybe RJ can pay to send you to one of those fancy boarding schools too. *And* he could hire you a personal psychotherapist to cure you of the voices in your head. Ha!"

Shaniya's still laughing when I press the end-call button, delete her name and number from my contacts and firmly switch my phone off. That done, I'm suddenly in shock, fingers trembling on the warm plastic. Back down in London, Shaniya will be blackly muttering about my usual sense-of-humour failure, I'm betting.

But I can now see what I haven't before: Shaniya's glaring, obvious kindness-failure. When I saw the way that bullying maid treated Flora earlier, I thought how awful it is that someone can have such power over you, that they can make a fool of you and talk to you like you're dirt.

And all this time, that's what's been happening to *me*.

I realize with a stab to the heart that for so long – way too long – I've put up with the *worst* best friend a girl could have. How could I have let that happen? Probably 'cause I didn't have much choice; the other girls we hung around with at school weren't *really* my friends ... when I think about it, they barely spoke to me if Shaniya wasn't around.

Dabbing at my streaming eyes with the sleeves of my jumper, I'm swamped with a sense of loneliness – and the realization that there's nothing to go back to London for. With no close family there and no friends to miss, my ties to my home town are properly, totally cut. So hey, it seems that I'm stuck here in Scotland, in weird-and-not-wonderful

Wilderwood Hall, in the middle of nowhere, with no one.

Well, perhaps there *is* someone. And she's not so very far away, just around the corner in the *other* Wilderwood. . .

Day Three at Wilderwood Hall and I'm staring at a toilet.

"Ha! How appropriate is that?" Mr Fraser laughs, kneeling on the bathroom floor, pointing at his paint-splattered portable radio with his screwdriver. The track playing is ABBA's "Waterloo". I smile. It's pretty funny.

"Anyway, the Edwardians were very interested in modernization," Mr Fraser goes back to telling me as he works at freeing the reluctant nuts and bolts of the old-fashioned loo in the main house's bathroom. Downstairs I can hear his crew clattering and banging away in the not-very-grand reception rooms.

"All mod cons, they liked, if they could afford it," he carries on. "So you see, this place's original owner – this Mr Richards with all his money – when he had this house designed he included the bathroom here, AND an indoor toilet in the servants' quarters, which must've seemed like luxury itself to the staff."

I feel a flutter in my tummy when I think of one member of Mr Richards' staff in particular... From what I've seen so far, Flora didn't exactly enjoy much luxury in her young life. How many coal scuttles did she have to lug up the back stairs every day to the housemaids' closet and beyond? How many fires did she have to build in all those rooms? How many chamber pots – yuck! – was she expected to carry and empty and clean? Actually, that gets me thinking of a question I could ask Mr Fraser.

"Would people in those days still use chamber pots as well as a proper toilet, if they had one?" I ask.

"Oh, yes. I've read a bit about that period, before the First World War," Mr Fraser chats cheerily, which is kind of surreal considering his face is so close to a loo that's more than a century old. "You can imagine that some of the household would be wary of new inventions, new ways."

I wonder if – back in the early 1900s – Mr Richards had pushed for all these newfangled features in the house, while Mrs Richards eyed them with suspicion.

"In fact," Mr Fraser continues, "plenty of folk actually thought it was completely unhygienic to have a toilet indoors at all! Isn't that amazing to think of?"

"I guess it is," I mutter, nodding in agreement.

Yes, amazing that some posh lady of the house might consider it unhygienic to have proper plumbing in the house, but would think nothing of her humble housemaid having to deal with other people's wee and poo on a daily basis.

"What about baths like these?" I say, looking at the huge, free-standing roll-top bath with its giant claw feet and chunky taps. "Were they quite a new idea too?"

"Yep," Mr Fraser answers with a grunt, as the nut he's trying to unscrew resists. "Folk were used to having tin baths in front of the fire. Some thought bathrooms were too draughty to be, you know, naked in. They thought it wasn't best for the health of little children."

Instantly I picture Flora lugging endless heavy

jugs of water upstairs for the little boy's bath by the fire. At least she was better off than maids who came before her, who'd have to fill baths for the grown-ups too. . .

"So, still no one else up, then?" Mr Fraser asks, changing the conversation.

He knows there's not. It was me – toast in hand by my bedroom window at eight a.m. this morning – who spotted the two vans crunching up to a halt and hurried to let Mr Fraser and his team in. In fact, I hurried so much that I knocked my phone off the windowsill, and didn't stop to check if it was cracked or broken. (What was the point? I had no one to call anyway. . .) And once I'd shyly ushered Mr Fraser and Co. inside, I even made them all mugs of coffee. Mum would be proud of me, if she wasn't still lost in snooze-land now.

"Nope," I reply, leaning on the door frame.

Yesterday, after the disastrous guided tour, Weezy stomped off to her room. She only reappeared for a mostly frosty meal in the evening, eaten on our knees in front of a laptop playing a DVD of *Modern Family*, since we couldn't get any reception for the TV. Weezy obviously wasn't a fan of *Modern Family*, or possibly *my* small branch of extended family, and after she'd finished her pizza and salad she scuttled back to the spare room. Mum deserted me pretty soon after, muttering something about needing to go over work in the office and try and call RJ. Again.

Which left me half-heartedly eating a lukewarm slice of pizza and wondering how on earth I'd ended up with a such a weird, uncomfortable "modern family" of my own.

A while later, after I'd brushed my teeth and switched my light out, I heard the buzz of Mum's voice on the phone, talking to RJ. Who knows what time of night the two of them stayed up talking till. . . ?

"That other girl; relative, is she?" Mr Fraser asks warily.

"Something like that," I reply. "She's my stepfather's daughter. From his first marriage."

"Ah. The two of you not get on, then?"

I can see why Mr Fraser would assume that, because of the silence in his van when he gave us both a lift from the Cairn Café.

"Yesterday was the first time I met her," I tell Mr Fraser.

He shoots me a look, a look that tells me he's pretty shocked by that fact but is too polite to say so. And now I worry that I've said too much. He'll probably sit down at tea tonight and tell his wife and his bird-eyed son all about the weird family living in Wilderwood. Then Cam will go off and tell whatever friends he has, and in a couple of weeks, after the holidays, I'll end up the awkward outsider at my new school, same as I was at my old one.

"Oh, I was supposed to tell you something," says Mr Fraser through his teeth, his jaw clenched with the effort of trying to slacken the nut. "I was talking to my wife about this place –"

I knew it. I *knew* we were gossip material.

"– and she remembered a conversation she had with the old couple that used to run the café in the village before they retired. They said that the hippy fella that once owned Wilderwood back in the 1970s; he didn't leave 'cause he ran out of money. It was more that he went a bit mad with the loneliness, apparently. The last time he dropped by the café he told them – actually, I probably shouldn't say."

"Yes, you should. *Please* tell me," I urge him, dying to find out some snatch of the house's history.

Of course, as soon as the internet is up and

running, I can hopefully find out more, but any crumb of information will do for now.

"All right," says Mr Fraser, fixing his eyes on me. "But it's probably a load of rubbish, so promise this isn't going to give you nightmares, or the wife won't forgive me."

"Promise," I say with a smile, to show how sensible I am.

"Well, this hippy fella says he's packing up and leaving 'cause he can't get a decent night's sleep. For months he's been having these wild dreams about the house being flooded with seawater... See what I mean? Crazy stuff. Like I say, loneliness must have got to him."

"Must've," I agree.

OK, so now I can put a line through any interest in the ex-owner of Wilderwood. Dreams of the sea lapping at the floorboards of the servants' quarters have nothing to do with my own mad meanderings into the past.

"Aargh!" Mr Fraser suddenly roars, glowering at the rusted-in toilet fixings. "This is *not* working. I'm off to grab some WD-40 from the van. Back in a minute!"

I shift aside to let Mr Fraser stomp by in his heavy

work boots, while idly wondering what exactly WD-40 might be. But now that I have this room to myself, I move around it and run my hand over the rim of the huge sink, trying to imagine it fitting into our tiny shower room back in London.

And the bath ... All of a sudden, just for fun, I step into it and lie down, picturing myself luxuriating in warm water with froths of bubbles. 'Cause with my eyes closed, it's easy to imagine it featuring in some ad for shampoo or chocolate or something, chilled-out music noodling in the background.

And just then, White Star Line's single begins to play on Mr Fraser's tinny little radio! I hum along to the verse, with my eyes still closed against the tattiness of the bathroom, feeling glad that Mr Fraser isn't here to spot the way my cheeks flushed at the sound of RJ's track.

The thing is, Mr Fraser doesn't know that his direct employer is the singer in a well-known band, and that's the way it should stay till the work's done, the estate agent advised, otherwise tradesmen might put their prices up. But Mr Fraser seems nice. I bet he wouldn't do something like that. He seems too friendly and down-to-earth.

"And when your world isn't turning and your path leads nowhere, don't be scared, keep on walking, turn the corner, I'll be there. . ." I croon softly, while my mind meanders on to what Mr Fraser just told me; the strange imaginings of the hippy who lived here. Did he dream of his bed bobbing as waves washed down the corridor? Or seaweed tangling itself round the legs of his armchairs. . . ?

It takes me a second or two to realize something has changed.

The radio has gone silent. But through the cold enamel of the bath I can feel a deep, insistent vibration. I don't know if I'm scared or thrilled. But what I *do* know is that I'm suddenly lying, floating in warm water. *Real* warm water.

With a start, I open my eyes, and see Flora standing in the middle of the large bathroom, looking back at me, just as startled. Over one arm she has a pile of fluffy white towels. And in the other hand, she is holding a blue glass bottle. She has it lifted to her lips, as if she's about to drink it, like Alice in Wonderland. But she's Flora in Wilderwood and was probably just smelling some expensive potion belonging to whoever was supposed to be having this bath. . .

"What are you doing in there?" she says in a panic.

I sit up in the bath, water pouring from my clothes. There are no bubbles, so when I look down I can see the submerged deep blue of my jeans.

"I – I don't know," I tell her, feeling flustered. "But it's all right. Remember, only *you* can see me."

Glancing around, I spot a pristine loo, with a polished wooden seat that doesn't exist in *my* version of the Hall.

"But why would you even step into the mistress's bath?" Flora asks, still dumbfounded, seeing me so unexpectedly.

"There wasn't any water when I got in," I say. "I – I was just lying here listening to music and –"

"– and you were singing!" says Flora. "When I came in just now with the towels, the bath was run and waiting for the mistress. *You* were not here. And then I looked up at the sound of your voice, and there you were!"

I have no idea what to do. Do I get out, soaking wet, or stay where I am till I'm called back to my own time? But what if I stay put, and Mrs Richards walks in, chucks off her dressing gown and climbs in here with me?

It's such a ridiculous idea that I start laughing. Properly laughing. Laughing like I haven't done in weeks. In months. I'm laughing so much it's infectious, and now Flora joins in.

She laughs so much that she spills some of the potion from the blue bottle on to the perfectly tiled floor – which makes us both laugh even more. We're still laughing when the door flies open and a young woman I've never seen flies in.

"Are you completely deranged, Flora Dean?" she barks.

Her outfit is similar to Flora's except that the dress is grey instead of black, and looks newer and less worn. The twists of plaited hair around her head are more ornate than I suspect Flora would be allowed.

"Pardon, but I had a fit of the sneezes," says Flora, giving a tiny, polite curtsy to the young woman.

"No you did not; you were *laughing!*" the young woman accuses her.

"No, Miss Ann, that's not how it was," says Flora, her eyes to the floor and her expression far from funny. "But I have been told I have the most peculiar sneezes."

At Flora's quickly thought excuse, I lose it and

burst out laughing again. Then I grip the bath and check for a reaction – luckily this Miss Ann, the ladies' maid – has no clue that I exist. But poor Flora, her cheek is twitching as she struggles to keep her composure.

"So you're mocking me, are you?" Ann says snidely. "I warn you, I'm watching you, Flora. One slip and you'll be out of here so fast. Don't think I can't guess who put horse manure on my shoe yesterday afternoon, and let me walk it all along the landing and into milady's room!"

"I would not do that!" Flora protests, her cheeks flaming. "Why would I, since I was called for to clean it?"

Poor Flora... I might feel alone in my world, but she is *beyond* alone, facing these bullying older workmates without any family or friends to turn to. Though she has *me* now, I remind myself, feeling a flurry of protectiveness towards her.

"You're such a sly creature I wouldn't ever say I could understand your ways," hisses Ann, snatching the towels and the bottle from Flora, who gasps, as if Ann's cutting words are a slap.

I watch, held back by the weight of water, as Flora flings the bathroom door wide open and makes her escape . . . straight through Weezy.

"Oh!" exclaims my so-called step-sister, her eyes blinking behind her black geek glasses.

My mind flips from one time to another, and I realize Weezy is gasping at the sight of a girl sitting fully dressed in an empty bath, and not because a servant from a bygone time slipped into the past through her tall, tomboyish, modern-day body.

"Sorry, I just thought I'd see how comfy it was," I quickly say, getting up on to my haunches, ready to propel myself out of the tub.

Weezy stands staring, her long red hair ruffled with bed-head tangles.

"Whatever," she mutters, as if what I say, think or do is of zero interest to her. "Does this stuff work?"

She's pointing to the loo, sink and the bath I'm clambering out of.

"I – I think it will do soon. Mr Fraser is fixing it all up today."

"Good. This'll be my bathroom, then. And I'm moving to that big corner room. The one I'm in now is too depressing. . ."

Weezy turns and goes without another word.

By the time I'm out of the bath, I can hear her dragging something out of Flora's room and out through the connecting door of the East Wing.

"Do you need a hand?" I ask, realizing she's pulling the heavy futon mattress across the landing towards the old nursery.

"No," Weezy replies flatly.

All I can do is lean on the doorway of the bathroom and watch as this tall, spiky cuckoo makes herself quite at home in my nest. . .

"Whoops!" says Mum, and nearly goes flying.

Her white Converse trainers might have been perfectly fine for padding from our London flat to the Tube and back, but for a walk in a stony and muddy Scottish forest, they're pretty awful. Mum does have some wellies packed somewhere – from when we went to the Latitude festival last summer – but she doesn't know which of the still-taped-up boxes they're stashed in.

"Got you," I say, making a grab for the arm of Mum's sky-blue Puffa jacket and steadying her. "It can't be much further now. I think I can hear water."

"Must be. Gordon the builder said it's just a five-minute walk from the car park to the pool," Mum chats away, though her eyes, like mine, are fixed on Weezy stomping ahead of us in her beanie, parka and flowery Doc Marten boots. "Can't wait to check out first local attraction!"

Today is amazingly sunny and warm for April, and so if we were normal tourists it would be the perfect time for sightseeing in the Highlands. But our weird little group – me, Mum, and a sulky eighteen-year-old stranger – aren't exactly normal tourists.

And the only reason Mum decided to do this really is because there are about a dozen different sets of drilling going on back at the Hall, and the noise was like finding yourself locked in a steel drum with a bunch of metal ball bearings and being pushed down a hill. I think Mr Fraser felt bad, and suggested the outing to Mum, drawing a map to the Linn o' Glenmill on the back of an envelope. So here we are.

"Mum, are you OK with Weezy moving into that room in the main house?" I ask, dropping my voice, though Weezy's too far ahead to hear me.

"Well, there's dust everywhere and the builders are storing some tools in there . . . but if she's happy to camp out in it for now, I guess that's fine by me," says Mum.

"For now?" I repeat hopefully. "For now" doesn't sound too long.

"Listen, I still don't know what's happening, Ellis," Mum answers, sounding tired. "RJ is trying to sort things out with Beth, which is never easy at the best of times. But the idea is that he wants to persuade Weezy to get back to boarding school after the holidays. It's what's best for her."

A dark thought bobs into my mind . . . Shaniya "joked" about RJ sending me off to boarding school too. Just as quickly I shake it out of my head, remembering we're talking about Weezy here, not me.

"Hey, did you ever find out why she got so angry at the stable block yesterday?" I take the opportunity to ask Mum.

I know Weezy wouldn't say what was wrong when Mum followed her and caught her up at the ivy-covered fountain. So the flip-out over the star tattoo stayed a mystery . . . unless Mum had got her to talk about it since.

"I spoke to RJ about it when you guys were in bed last night," she tells me. "He got his white star tattoo done on tour in Amsterdam last year. Weezy joined him over there for the weekend and went with him to watch. He told her it would always remind him of her..."

"But now it's a you-and-him thing," I say, suddenly getting why Weezy might feel put out. Or *shoved* out.

"I guess. Anyway, come on, we'd better not lose her, or RJ'll never forgive me!" Mum says with a smile, speeding up as Weezy disappears from view over the brow of a wooded hillock. With a scurry and a scramble we end up coming to an opening in the forest . . . and it's completely beautiful.

The dense clutch of trees has thinned out and directly in front of us is a high outcrop of granite. A waterfall gushes and splashes over it, flowing down into a huge circular pool in the rocks. The water then rushes and darts noisily over boulders, and becomes a stream that turns into a river that runs towards Glenmill village and then off on its journey to the faraway sea. (Which way, which sea, I wonder, since we're right in the middle of Scotland, as far from the Atlantic as we are from the North Sea.)

Weezy is staring at the view, and then down at an information board planted in the ground. It only takes me and Mum a few steps to get to her side.

"This is a bit special, isn't it?" says Mum.

Weezy, as usual, doesn't bother to reply.

"What does the board say, Weezy?" Mum asks as she pulls her jacket off now we're hot from the walk.

"It says 'linn' is old Scots for *pool*," Weezy mutters, idly drawing her index finger along the dusty lines of information on the metal board. "And the pool is an almost perfect circular basin, carved out of the rock by water during the last Ice Age..."

Wow. That's more words than I've ever heard her say, put together.

"Ha! That puts time into perspective, doesn't it?" says Mum. "It makes an old place like Wilderwood Hall seem as modern-day as the Shard!"

My mood lightens at Mum's mention of the Shard. She took me there as a surprise for my thirteenth birthday back in December, and I remember my shock, standing under this towering high-rise central London office block that looks like a giant glass splinter fallen from space. "We're going up *there*?" I'd checked with her. "We sure are," she replied. "We get the lift all the way to the top, to the viewing platform." So that's what we did. And I blew out a candle on a cupcake while we looked at the jaw-dropping view of London with snowflakes gently drifting over it. . .

That sudden happy memory makes me realize something. Flora will have her *own* happy memories of London soon. And New York soon after.

I need to find her when I we get back today and make the most of her company before the family and staff head off on their grand adventure. . .

"Hey, is that a seal?" Mum suddenly asks, frowning at a shape that's just bobbed up in the middle of the pool.

"It can't be," I say, holding my hand above my eyes to shield them from the sun. "Seals live in the sea, not in—"

I stop dead mid-sentence at the sight of a hand lifting from the water.

If Flora was here by my side, she'd be claiming it as a selkie. But I know it's not a seal, or a selkie, or any other kind of animal, real or imagined. His messy hair might be lying flat and sleek against his head because of the water, but the waving boy happily gasping for breath after his underwater swim is Cam.

"Oh, it's Gordon's son," Mum exclaims happily, waving back at him. "That's nice. You girls can go chat to him while I try and, you know, sort stuff out."

My tummy instantly flips with irritation.

When Mum says "sort stuff out", she means try and get through to RJ again. Why does she need to track him down all the time? Won't he call when he can, when he's got anything to tell her about what's happening? Can't she just spend time with me?

We could sit by that picnic table over there and chat, and let *Weezy* talk to the seal boy...

"Oi, Bella! Joe!" Cam suddenly yells.

Who are they? I wonder. Friends from school?

But it's not human voices that answer him.

"Arf! Arf! Arf!!"

Scattershot barking bursts into the quiet of the scene, and me, Mum and Weezy watch in surprise as two tongue-lolling dogs come hurtling out of the woods and jump straight into the freezing pool. Cam laughs at his doggy-paddling pets, then begins to swim to us humans.

"Hey, more company for you and Weezy!" says Mum, patting me on the arm. "Go on over!"

I turn and give Mum a puppy-eyed look of desperation that I know she'll recognize as "Save me!"

But it seems she's not in the mood for doing any such thing. She's in the mood for staring down at her phone as if it's a lifeline, and heading over to the picnic table to be alone with it.

And so there's nothing much I can do, except start mooching over to the water's edge, where I settle myself cross-legged, feeling the prickles of pine needles niggling my bare ankles in the space between my jeans and socks. I scratch at the itchiness, just for something to do, as the splashing sounds from the water get louder and nearer.

But I can't ignore the "Hi!" that's said directly to me.

"Hello," I say to Cam, who's treading water.

One of the dogs is still happily swimming in steady circles, while the other one has scrambled out and starts shaking itself dry horribly close to me.

"I know you're Ellis," says Cam, "but who are you?"

Weezy must be standing right behind me, though I hadn't checked to see if she'd followed me over to the water.

"I'm Weezy," she replies, but doesn't give up any more information than that.

"Interesting name. And are you an interesting person?"

There's a sudden, surprising noise.

It's Weezy, bursting out laughing at this cheeky question.

"Well, let's see," she says, stepping forward so her flowery Doc Martens end up parked next to my crossed knee. "If you asked anyone I know, they'd probably say no."

"No? Well, they sound boring people themselves. I must remember never to meet them," Cam says with a grin.

"You won't. They're all at my boarding school," Weezy replies flatly.

"Is that Inverkellen? Just north of here?" asks Cam.

That's the name of the other school in the area, the one I saw on Google Maps when I was trying to spot Glenmill High.

"Nope. Mine's way, *way* down in the south of England, in Devon. But I'm not going back," Weezy announces, and I see her determinedly digging the heel of one boot into the ground to emphasize the fact.

Uh-oh, that won't be good news for RJ. I quickly glance over at Mum, but see that she's looking serious and staring at me.

It gives me the shivers.

I feel like I'm being discussed.

In fact, for all I know, Shaniya is right (for once) and RJ is at this moment trying to persuade Mum that the best option for me is a spell at Inverkellen boarding school. Then he'll have Mum all to himself when he comes back, won't he?

"OK, so now I know you're an *ex*-boarder. Tell me something else," I hear Cam continue with his cheerful interrogation of Weezy.

"Like what?" replies Weezy.

"Well, describe yourself in three words," says Cam.

"Nope," says Weezy, but the tone of her voice is edging on friendly.

"Ah, go on," Cam urges. "Everyone can do that. Here's mine: Glaswegian, drummer, idiot."

"Well, I can see *one* of those three is true," Weezy teases.

Mum sees me watching, and drops her eyes. (Ripples of anxiety start to rise.)

"You go first," I hear Weezy say, then realize she's talking to *me*, when her boot nudges up against my knee.

"I don't want to," I say, because I'm swamped

with sudden worries and nerves and all I can think of right now is "anxious, shy, mad", and I'm not prepared to say that out loud.

"OK," says Cam, who doesn't seem interested enough to push me for my list of three. "So, are you two coming in, then?"

"Coming in?" I hear myself bleat in a squeaky-with-surprise voice.

"Well, *yeah*," Cam laughs at me. "The Loch Ness Monster doesn't live in here, you know."

I can't stand that snidey, sarky sort of humour, even though I should be used to it, being "friends" with Shaniya for so long.

"I *know* that. I just don't want to, and anyway, I haven't got a swimsuit or a towel with—"

Cam has stopped looking at me. He's not even listening. He's too busy grinning at something happening right beside me.

Weezy's parka has just flopped on to the ground, followed by a black hoodie.

"OK, OK; I've got my three!" Weezy suddenly announces, and bizarrely tugs her loosely fastened boots off. "Giant."

She's making a joke about her height. Is she self-conscious about it too, like me? I wonder.

I don't wonder for long; I'm too confused by the fact that she's now peeling off both her black ankle socks. And in that second I see something on the inside of her wrist – a white star tattoo. It must be fairly recently done; the skin around it looks pink and a little sore. Whoa; no wonder she didn't like it when she saw Mum's.

Bent down now, Weezy's gaze meets mine – she knows I've seen. Her deep brown eyes seem to be daring me to say something about it, but I'm too shy and wary of her to say anything at all. So Weezy turns back towards Cam, her face becoming animated again as she calls out her next word.

"Failure."

What? Why's she said that?

But omigod, she's wriggling her jeans off now...

"SWIMMER!"

"Go, Go, GO!" chants Cam, and I feel a rush of air beside me as Weezy leaps from the rocky pool's edge – wearing only a black vest top and purple knickers – and hurtles herself into the water. Cam cheers her on, the dogs bark madly, and Mum, spotting what's gone on, whoops and applauds from the picnic bench.

As for me? I feel a dull, hard chill settle in my

chest. Even a practically silent, gloomy stranger can make herself at home here better than me.

I can't stand to look as Cam treads water by Weezy's side, laughing and congratulating her on her cannonball, while she grins and shrugs back at him, wiping tendrils of now dark red hair back from her face. You know, RJ and Mum might as well pack me off to boarding school, I think as I lean over and gaze down into the water, swirling it with my hand.

What is it about me that makes fitting in so difficult? Everyone else seems to find life so easy.

A while ago, Mum said it's because I haven't found my "tribe" yet. That I'll probably stop feeling so anxious when I meet people who are like me – and *like* me – and then I can relax. But I don't feel like that's going to happen anytime soon. And I can't even remember what it feels like to be totally relaxed. Even on good days, even hanging out with Mum, the waves are always just in sight, ready to roll in. . .

Then I remember this morning, laughing till I could hardly breathe with Flora. There were no waves then.

Oh, I wish I was back in Wilderwood, where I have one friend at least. . .

Then a sudden movement from below catches my eye. Something is lurking in the depths of the dark water. It's moving fast, rushing up towards me. A face. Just like the altered refraction I saw over the side of the boat, the day Mum married RJ.

"No, no, NO!" I scream as the face bursts out from the surface of the water, eyes locked on mine.

14

Headphones plugged in her ears, Weezy is sprawled on the back seat, her skin steaming through her leggings and hoodie as she dries off in the heat of the car. Her wet T-shirt, bra and knickers are bundled in a ball on the floor.

I think I totally freaked her out, screaming the way I did when she swam up under me. Apart from saying sorry at the pool, she hasn't said another word to me. She's probably wondering when the first train back to Somerset or boarding school is so she can get as far away from her unhinged stepsister as possible.

Mum, driving, looks quickly at me in the passenger seat and mouths "OK?"

We've all got headphones in. Mum's are connecting her to a call with RJ. Mine are connected to nothing at all. I shoved them in out of habit but I'm not in the mood for music.

Anyway, I nod a yes at Mum, and turn to stare out of the window at the green, wooded countryside zooming by. And then I realize I can still hear Mum's conversation, while she thinks I've tuned out.

"Hello? RJ? Can you speak? Sorry – it all got a bit mad back there."

"Sure." I can just make out the mumble of RJ's reply through her headset. He's a singer, after all. He can't help but boom. "Are her panic attacks getting worse, do you think?"

My heart lurches. My stepdad's voice might be faint, but when you're being talked about, it's like you have a special radar that locks in to the words on your behalf.

I'm well-trained in that, thanks to my crowd at school. Shaniya and the others were always commenting on the state of my hair, on how lame my school shoes were, how embarrassingly keen I was in class or anything else they could dissect about me.

So what I have has a name, according to RJ, and Mum too, presumably. I have panic attacks...?

Out of the corner of my eye I see Mum turn to check I'm not getting any of this. So I stay completely still, pretending I'm not.

"She'll be fine," says Mum. "Just give it a little time."

"But how much time?" I hear RJ say.

What does he mean "How much time?"

Did I guess right earlier? That RJ is going to spend a chunk of his money on sending me to Inverkellen as soon as I settle down and quit panicking? It might be why Mum's been having all these calls the last few days. Why I felt she's been a bit secretive with me. It's not ALL been about Weezy, has it? RJ doesn't seem to have a problem with packing his *own* daughter away, so why would he hesitate to do the same with me...?

(Here come the waves, here come the waves...)

"*Aaaarghh!*"

A sudden scream cuts through my rising, bubbling stress. What's happened? Is there a car coming on the wrong side? Has a deer jumped in front of the car? I whip around to face Mum and see that she's beaming with love and joy.

"YES!" she yelps, nearly losing control of the car on a corner.

Automatically, I put a hand out on the dashboard and brace myself, but Mum straightens the car up again.

"Baby, you're cutting out," Mum says urgently. "Say that again. When? RJ! RJ! Oh, he's gone. . ."

"What's wrong?" Weezy leans between the seats and asks.

"Nothing's wrong," Mum says, sounding giddy now. "Your dad's cancelled some dates on the band's promo tour. He's coming home, to Wilderwood. He's on his way now!"

It's like a switch tripped inside Weezy and her whole face lights up at the news. Mum is so happy she's crying. And I just go rigid and still, not knowing what to think or how to feel. . .

The switch in Weezy has stayed at "on". There's excitement in her eyes and a new softness in her face. Mum can see it too, and takes advantage of the moment.

"He's *so* looking forward to seeing you, Weezy," Mum says warmly as we clamber out of the car.

Weezy looks across at Mum and gives her a

sweet, nervous smile. It makes her look more like a six-year-old about to meet Santa in a department store grotto than the sulky girl we've had to put up with the last twenty-four hours.

"I'm *still* angry with him," says Weezy, though she doesn't look particularly angry any more.

"Well, feel free to shout at him when he gets here," Mum says cheerfully as she walks over to Weezy and risks slipping her arm around her waist. "It's a huge place with no neighbours, so yell as loud as you like..."

I watch, waiting for Weezy to shrug off Mum's arm, but she doesn't. Instead, she smiles again, wider this time, and she and Mum walk companionably towards the back door of the East Wing.

In that second, I feel almost invisible, a complete outsider in this unexpected bonding moment.

Well, if I'm an outsider, I might as well *stay* outside, I decide.

And the glint of light in the corner of my eye as I got out of the car just now settles it for me.

It might mean that Flora's near, or I'm close, depending on how this strange slither through time works.

"I'm just going to hang out here," I announce.

"Are you sure?" asks Mum, looking at me closely. "I was going to break out the cheesecake to celebrate the news!"

"I'll have some later," I tell her, and leave Mum and Weezy to go indoors. Mum hesitates, keys in hand, and shoots me a questioning look.

"I'm fine. Bit travel-sick. I'll get some air," I tell her, and walk off.

I'm alone at last, but it's not exactly peaceful. Even out here the drone of drills and crash of hammers disturbs the quiet of the gardens. But I try my best to blank out the noise as I amble along the short L of the East Wing, trailing my fingers along the rough stone wall, my eyes on the ivy-covered fountain up ahead. Wonderfully, I feel the whisperings in my fingers straight away.

"*You will not. . .*" a man's voice murmurs. "*You will not. . .*"

It grows louder and clearer as I walk, and I'm concentrating so hard I nearly trip over the girl huddled on the ground right in front of me, her back to the granite wall.

"Flora!" I say, righting myself and then dropping down beside her. "Is something wrong?"

Her arms are clasped tightly around her knees, so tightly her knuckles are white. When she raises her face to me she looks mad with grief.

"Mr Stewart has just this minute told me I'm not to go!"

"Mr Stewart?" I say. "Who is he again? And where are you not allowed to go?"

"He is the butler," Flora says, wiping her wet nose with the back of her hand. "He came past with a packing chest on the stairs and I took the chance to mention the trip to America, and to ask what we maids should pack for ourselves."

"And what did Mr Stewart say to that?" I ask her.

"He tells me that I misunderstood. That not *all* the household will go. That I will not go."

"Flora, no!" I gasp.

"Oh, yes. The others, they will all see London. All of them, right down to Minnie, because the mistress cannot do without Mrs Wallace to cook for the family – especially not in some foreign place, she says – and Mrs Wallace says she will not manage without her *Minnie*." Flora practically spits out that last name.

"And then they will sail together over the great

Atlantic Ocean. Minnie and Ann and Jean and the rest; they'll spend their half-days off wandering the streets of New York. . ."

"But why aren't you going along too?"

"Mr Stewart announced that a few staff must stay behind to maintain the house till the master and his family are back in three months' time," Flora says bitterly. "And so Mr Sykes the under-butler is to stay, but he is old and lazy and will hide away in his rooms drinking beer all day. And Mrs Strachan is to employ an elderly lady from the village to come and stay, and she is to help me clean all the rugs and carpets and linen while everyone is gone."

Flora's acute disappointment hangs like a cloud over her. I scan my brain, trying to think of something comforting to say.

"Well, at least you won't have *that* lot moaning at you all the time," I say, and am rewarded with a small, watery smile.

"Yes, I suppose that *is* something I should be glad for," says Flora, though it's obviously not much comfort to her.

"What about your parents? Or brothers and sisters?" I ask, hoping a mention of her family might cheer her up. I realize I know nothing of them. "Can you take some days off since the household is away, and go see them?"

"I've been home just once this last year. My family live too far away for me to visit," she says, roughly smearing the wetness from her face with her hands. "And I don't have the fare anyway; I must save my wages and send them to my parents to keep my little brothers and sisters fed and clothed. They're all Mother cares for; to her and my father, all I'm really good for is earning now that I'm grown."

How incredibly scary to have that responsibility at fourteen. I can't begin to imagine what a weight that must be and how isolated Flora must be all the time.

"Hey, it's not as bad as what *you're* going through," I say, settling myself down properly beside her, "but it makes you feel any better, I'm having a pretty miserable time where *I* come from."

"Why? Are people being cruel to you too?" asks Flora, setting aside her own unhappiness and gazing at me with real concern.

But where do I start? I think about telling her everything, like my new, niggling worry that RJ might try and persuade Mum to send me away, and about Weezy arriving here, like a storm cloud. Or how Shaniya broke my confidence into tiny little pieces over the course of Year Eight. I even think about telling Flora the story of my runaway dad and the uselessness of my distant (in both senses of the word) grandmother. Instead, I realize there's one quick, shortcut way to tell her how I feel.

"I'm just so lonely."

"But do you not live with your mother?" asks Flora.

"Yes," I say, picturing my lovely mum, with her new secrets and her new husband. "But my mother has remarried. And it feels like I'm losing her. . ."

Shaniya would've snorted at this point, telling me to get real and not be so dramatic. She'd make her clever, sharp digs about me being spoiled. But I'm not talking in London, and I'm not with Shaniya, thank goodness. I'm with Flora. And even though she doesn't know the version of the world I come from, she seems to understand me.

"We're both the same," says Flora, lifting a skinny arm from around her knees and wrapping it around my shoulders instead. "We're *both* lonely. But we don't have to be any more. Not now we've found each other."

She gently rests her head against mine. I close my eyes and my shoulders sink as the stress leaves them. It feels so good to think I might have found a true friend in this strange place, in this strange way.

"Can you sing me that song?" Flora asks in a quiet voice. "The one you were singing this morning? It reminds me of my shadow dream. . ."

My mind is so scattered with all that's happened in the last few days that it takes me a second to think what she's talking about. And then I remember, and begin to softly murmur the words to "Turn the Corner".

Right now I might not be too sure about the man who wrote these lyrics, but the words themselves seem pretty perfect for me and Flora. By the second time I sing the chorus, she knows it and begins to harmonize in a sweet high voice.

"*Turn the corner. . .*"

"*There I'll stand. . .*"

"*Turn the corner. . .*"

"*Take my hand. . .*"

"*Turn the corner. . .*"

"*Don't be scared. . .*"

"Turn the corner. . ."

"I'll be there!"

As our voices fade, the waves seem so far away I can barely feel them. . .

Till the shrill screech of a drill shakes me awake, and I'm just a girl, sitting on a cold stone slab, all by herself.

"He's here! HE'S HERE!" Mum yells from somewhere in the East Wing.

And then I make out the pattering of feet as she – and Weezy? – hurry down the back stairs.

But I already know RJ's arrived, because I'm at my bedroom window and have just watched the dark-windowed hire car turn and slowly crunch to a stop in the parking place by the old stables.

Well, I guess the secret of who the true owner of the house is will be well and truly out pretty soon. Day Four at Wilderwood Hall and the gossip will start, 'cause some of Mr Fraser's work crew are bound to recognize RJ, or possibly even be big fans of White Star Line.

As soon as the car stops and the engine dies, the driver's-side door creaks open, and I see Mum running, hurling herself into RJ's open arms. And then RJ spots Weezy, who's standing there, shuffling awkwardly. But she crumbles the second he waves her over to him, and soon they're lost in a hug too.

A three-way hug, I notice, as RJ kisses the tops of both Mum's and Weezy's heads. From where I'm standing, it looks like my ice-princess stepsister might be thawing... I know I should go and say hello. But before I can make a move, I see that the passenger door of the car has opened too. Who is it? I wonder to myself. Did one of the other band members come back with RJ? Or his personal assistant, perhaps?

I look, I squint, and I see that it's a boy. In fact, it's Cam...

Cam?!

Ripples.

Waves.

Confusion.

The feelings all crash and rush inside me as I head out into the corridor and listen to the jumble of voices and footsteps thundering up the back stairs.

RJ's leading the way, appearing tall and rangy in front of me in his skinny jeans, black T-shirt, dark grey suit jacket and stripy scarf.

"Well, hello, hello, Ellis!" he says, beaming at me and holding out the wide arc of his arms. "How's my little London lady doing in the wilds of Wilderwood?"

I'm all ready to be brittle with him, not to fall for his famous-musician charm. But before I know it, RJ has rushed over and lifted me clean off the floor, and I can't help but give a surprised shriek of delight. It's actually nice to feel small sometimes, or for the first time in for ever, really.

And then my smile fades as I glance over RJ's shoulder and catch sight of the expression on Weezy's face. From that shocked, death-ray glare I can tell that even if she's starting to warm a little to Mum, *I'm* still the enemy, as far as she's concerned. . . The damage might be done, but I instantly wriggle myself free from RJ's hug and step back.

"So," he says, letting me go. "I can't wait for you to show me around this place. Are you up for being my tour guide, Miss Harper?"

"Uh, sure," I say, feeling flattered but flustered by RJ's attention. "Where do you want to start?"

I'm thrown by how kindly and friendly he seems, and how unexpectedly pleased I am to see him.

How stupid am I being? Am I *that* desperate for attention at the moment that I can happily push aside worries of the secret conversations he and Mum have been having lately?

"Hold on; not just yet, love," RJ interrupts my thoughts. "Give's a while. I've just got to get a couple of important things sorted first."

And so I press the stop button on my enthusiasm, feeling it quickly drain away. Of *course* there's stuff that's more important than me. I think I'm pretty much always bottom of everyone's list of important stuff, even Mum's at the moment. For her, RJ, the Shiny New Project and Weezy rank at one, two and three, with me trailing in fourth – and last – position.

"And one of those is an overdue heart-to-heart with *this* gorgeous girl," says RJ, turning to Weezy, who beams back at him. "But before *that*, I really need to look at what you've got there, Cam. . ."

For a second or two, I'd forgotten all about Mr Fraser's son. But there he is, right behind Mum. He's holding a newspaper, I notice. Is that what he's come to show us?

"This is the living room. Let's go in here," says Mum, ushering everyone into the room – including Cam.

As I follow him inside, I sneak a sideways peek at him. How did he end up getting a lift from RJ, I wonder? And does he even realize who RJ actually *is*? Probably not, or he'd be looking more shell-shocked, I think.

"So come on, let's see it properly," says RJ, frowning as he plonks himself down on the sofa.

"You can spread it out here," Mum tells Cam, and points to the low coffee table. Cam tries to do what he's told, rustling his way through the pages as he looks for something specific.

"What's going on?" I ask as I perch on the arm of the sofa.

"We're not exactly alone here at Wilderwood, *that's* what," says Weezy.

My jaw drops. She's not . . . she can't be talking about Flora, can she?

"Don't be scared, Ellis," Mum jumps in quickly, spotting the shocked look on my face. "RJ spotted Cam with his bike, not far from ours. He'd had a puncture and –"

"– and I stopped to help," RJ continues. "But

it turned out he was cycling *here*, to show your mum *this*."

Cam's finally managed to open the newspaper where he wants it.

And there, in the Entertainment section, are some words in a heavy, black, unmissable font.

RJ Johnstone's Scottish Love Nest. Under the heading are several photos that have clearly been taken right here, in the grounds of Wilderwood Hall.

Waves roll in as I stare at an image of me and Mum on the terrace, the morning after we moved in, me hunched and tired after my endless sleep. And here's another, of Mum on the phone, pacing the terrace. The third – and largest – is of her sitting on the terrace clutching a mug, looking forlorn. *Marriage not all it's cracked up to be, Mrs Johnstone?* says the jokey caption underneath.

Another, a small inset in the corner, was taken just yesterday, I realize. It's of Mum and Weezy looking like they're arguing by the ivy-tangled fountain. The stable block – and a figure that's me – is in the background. So the paparazzi have been busy again, though this time they've been stealthier than it was possible to be on the noisy speedboat on the Thames. . .

"I can't believe this! Where were these taken from?" Weezy asks angrily.

Maybe I've been feeling a little pushed out of this family, but at least I can be useful in this instance.

"I think I know. Here, I'll show you," I say.

Pushing myself off the arm of the sofa, I walk out into the corridor. Everyone follows behind me – Pied Piper style – as I go through the panelled linking door, across the first floor landing of the main house and into the corner bedroom; the original nursery, as only *I* know it, and where Weezy has loosely set up camp, to everyone else.

"I think the photographer has to have been over there somewhere, to get those angles. Maybe hiding behind those trees and bushes by the far wall. . . ?"

"Yeah!" Cam chips in. "When I spoke to you yesterday, Ellis, there was a flash from that direction. It must've been sunlight catching on the lens."

I'm glad to be helpful, but part of me is withering with disappointment. Each time I saw those fleeting glimmers of lights, it *hadn't* been a tiny portal into the past like I'd hoped. Instead it was just some cash-hungry photographer, snooping around.

"So this bloke's just walked right in, because the gates are wedged open," says Mum, gazing at the entrance to the grounds.

"You need to get my dad to fix them so they lock," Cam suggests. "Maybe get an intercom with a video screen. Dad fitted one of those for that TV chef that's got a place near here. *And* that comedian bloke with the beard. . ."

So *that's* why Cam didn't look particularly fazed by getting a lift here by the lead singer of White Star Line. I get the feeling he and his dad and possibly everyone around Glenmill knew all along who the new owner of Wilderwood was, and weren't that bothered, not if they're used to famous faces already.

"Gates or not, it's not on. This is private property," says RJ. "And it's crazy, really; I'm not famous enough to deserve this attention. It's especially not fair on you, honey."

RJ tenderly stokes Mum's scrunched-up blonde hair, and she circles her arms around his waist.

"Maybe he's out there right now, watching us!" says Weezy, shoving her slipping glasses back up on to her nose.

"Could be. Which is why I'm going out there – see if I can catch him, or scare him away," RJ announces.

"No you are not! That'll just make the situation loads worse!" says Mum, clinging on tight to RJ's waist. "Can you imagine if the photographer got a picture of you coming for him? The newspapers would LOVE that, wouldn't they?"

As the ranting and raving and discussion continues around me at full volume, I notice everyone's voices are beginning to fade. A new sound is slowly building. It's because my hands are resting on the windowsill, which felt warm to the touch a second ago, thanks to the afternoon sun seeping into the wood. But now it's cooling fast, and the fizz and crackles of some *different* voice is seeping into the palms of my hands, prickling up my fingers and forearms like sparkles of frost.

"*Stupid . . . stupid . . . stupid. . .*" the voice buzzes, till I sense the change.

I spin around and see Mum, RJ, Weezy and Cam, freeze-framed in the moment and fading from me. And the musty, dusty corner room as I know it fades too, replaced instead by the warmth and colour of the old nursery, busy with bookshelves, toys, a small tin bath, a globe and a blackboard on an easel.

And then there's a wooden rocking horse – complete with an impressive mane and tail of real horsehair – which sits by the small roaring fire.

Some kind of catastrophe has just occurred.

"You stupid girl!" a woman is shouting at Flora.

"Catriona, I—"

"I leave you to look after young Master Archibald for two minutes, just *two minutes*, and you let him do *this*?"

The woman doing the shouting is short and plump and might be pretty if she didn't look so flustered and furious. I try and think who she must be . . . Catriona; is she the nursemaid?

"He – he must have taken the poker when I was dusting the ashes from the fireplace," Flora insists, tears brimming in her eyes. "He was so very quiet I did not see him take it or see what he was doing!"

It's hard to hear what either Flora or Catriona is saying due to the wailing of the small boy who is currently brandishing a fire poker in his hand. And now I can clearly see what he's done; there are uneven scorch lines all down the side of the expensive-looking rocking horse.

"She said I could! She said I could!" the boy screams, pointing an accusing finger at Flora.

"No, no, I did not!" Flora gasps in horror, lifting her apron to hide her face in shock at this awful

186

accusation. "How can such a little boy tell such a lie?"

"Never mind that – what am I to tell his papa when he sees this damage?" says Catriona, her face crimson with rage and worry. "The master might try to dock my wages for this, you stupid—"

"What on *earth* is going on here?"

With a swish of heavy cloth and a tap of smart black boots, Miss Matilda the governess swoops into the room, drifting her floral scent after her. The gold rim of the cameo brooch at her neck glints in the flickering light of the nursery fire.

Straight away she sees the nursemaid opening and shutting her mouth like a panicked goldfish; Archibald clutching the heavy, hot poker; the vandalized rocking horse; and a trembling and distraught Flora. Without letting anyone babble, accuse or talk, Miss Matilda takes the situation in hand.

"Master Archibald, put that poker back in its place this instant. Catriona, please wash the coal dust off his hands immediately. Flora, can you please ask the housekeeper if she has some wood polish or oil that might help restore or disguise these marks."

Flora, glad of the escape, bobs politely, and – grabbing her half-filled coal scuttle – makes a speedy exit from the room. I hurry after her, weaving carefully past the nursemaid, the governess and the boy, though of course I could probably just as easily rush right through them for all the effect my twenty-first-century self would have on them.

Once out on the landing, with its pretty honeysuckle wallpaper and rich long rugs, I see Flora at the door of the housemaid's closet, holding it open for me. Out of habit, and forgetting that she alone can see me, I glance one way and another before slipping into the glorified cupboard with my friend.

Flora clunks the scuttle wearily down on the floor beside tall empty water jugs. Shelves line the walls, holding scrubbing brushes and cleaning rags and bottles and tins that must be cleaning products, I suppose. Two low, rectangular white sinks stand side by side in front of a small window, and it's against one of these deep sinks that Flora rests herself.

"You see how it is. They *all* have it in for me, Ellis!" she rails, her eyes wide, her expression desperate. "From Mrs Strachan down to the young master. If it's not Jim the stable lad claiming he saw me trip Minnie in church, it's Jean claiming the dead mouse in her bed was *my* work. Last week the master's dog died, and the gardener claimed he saw me put rat poison in the bowl of slops that was left for the dog at the back door! For saying such a thing, I wish I worked directly in the kitchen and could slip rat poison in the *gardener's* dinner. . ."

Flora's sudden spark of black humour gives me hope that she can keep her spirits up in this drab and difficult environment. But I hold back the smile, in case she thinks I'm laughing at her.

"Is there really no one at all that is ever kind to you?" I ask instead.

"There is not a kind person in this whole fine building, upstairs or down," Flora says with a heavy sigh. "*Everyone* in this house constantly finds fault with me, or blames me for things that are broken or lost, or simply thinks the worst of me. There is not one person in this entire place I can call my friend."

"You *know* that isn't true, Flora, not now," I remind her.

Flora's gaunt face suddenly brightens, and her brown eyes fill with hope. "To think I saw you in my dreams as a shadow, yet you are like my one true light in this dark place!"

"I really don't know about the dream part," I say, walking over to join her by the sinks with a smile and a shrug. "But I'm glad I make a difference. I just wish I could be around more for you."

"Oh, so do I!" says Flora, taking both my hands in hers. "Wouldn't that be grand?"

It's lovely to see her so comforted by the idea. But the hope and happiness in my *own* heart suddenly dims – and Flora sees that.

"What?" she asks. "What is it, Ellis?"

"I – I might be wrong, but I think my mother and her new husband might be thinking of sending me away to a boarding school," I tell her as I lean back against the other of the two deep, low sinks.

"No!" Flora gasps, squeezing my hands more tightly between hers. "They can't do that!"

I see the rising panic in her eyes and instantly regret telling her.

"Look, it might not happen," I say quickly, as much to comfort myself as Flora. "They haven't said anything to me. And if they did, I would just say . . . I would just say *no*, I'm not going."

"And they couldn't force you to?" asked Flora, amazed and surprised that a girl of my age could say such a thing to her elders.

"No, absolutely not," I assure her.

At the same time I wonder what will become of Weezy ... will *she* end up being persuaded to go back to her school in Devon? And if she is, what chance do *I* have of getting out of it? But I don't want to think about that right now. Flora's situation is *so* much worse than mine and I don't want to add to her unhappiness. So I try and think of something *else* to say that might be positive.

"Hey, you know, the governess doesn't seem as bad as the others," I point out, thinking that Miss Matilda sounded quite strict but fair. I mean, she didn't take the side of the spoilt little boy either time he was whining about Flora and trying to get her into trouble.

My friend's face darkens at that, though.

"Miss Matilda may not snap at me the way the others do, but she is nasty in her own way; she looks down her nose at me, as if I am nothing. As worthless as ashes."

I'm sorrier than ever for Flora. I might feel like I'm on the outskirts of my mum's life at the moment, but I'm reminded again of how Flora really is utterly, *scarily* alone. And for a fleeting second, that makes me think about Wilderwood itself, standing empty and unloved for so many decades. What happened to it? Apart, of course, from the hippy bloke in the 1970s with his strange dreams of the sea lapping at the skirting boards.

More importantly, what happened to Mr Richards, the first owner of the Hall? Did he simply get bored and abandon the place for some exciting new prospect? Maybe he saw business opportunities in America, when the family went to visit, and never returned to the UK.

I really, *really* need to research this once we get an internet connection. 'Cause if I can find out more about the house and the Richards family, maybe I can find out what happened to their staff too...

Then suddenly, unexpectedly, I notice that while my mind whirled with thoughts of Wilderwood and its inhabitants, Flora's expression has switched from sorrow to a knowing smile.

"You might not want to sit there, Ellis," she says, her eyes sparkling with mischief.

"Why not?" I ask warily, turning to look down at the clean, empty and innocent-looking porcelain sink.

"That's the one I use to empty the chamber pots..."

Instantly, I jump away in horror, then join in with Flora's giggles.

I'm still giggling when there's a sudden tugging at my back, and I find myself lurching away from Flora, my hands slipping out of hers, as if I'm being pulled by elastic ropes.

And then I'm floating free and fast, doors and walls a blur until I feel the warm wood of the nursery windowsill under my hands, and hear the familiar voices of Mum, RJ and the others, their excited chat continuing just as it had before I slipped and slid into that other Wilderwood.

So yes, I'm back home.

Though I suppose I wasn't ever really away. . .

Three's company, four's a crowd. It seems that way right now, as RJ strides through the wind-nipped village streets, with Mum linked into his right arm and Weezy linked into his left.

"Come on, Ellis!" Mum says over her shoulder, waving me to join in with her free hand.

"I'm fine," I say.

But Mum halts the threesome to let me catch up anyway.

"Hey, how cute is that, huh?" says RJ, using the pause to point at a little cottage I hadn't noticed before.

It's right behind the bench by the bus stop where I sat shivering the other day, till Moira the waitress motioned me to come inside the Cairn Café. The tiny house is low, just one storey high. RJ might think it's cute, but he'd never be able to stand up in it.

In the panel of glass above the front door the name *Honeysuckle Cottage* is painted in faded gold lettering, while bare rose branches ramble haphazardly over the walls, the blooms hidden for now but ready to appear with a pop when spring turns to summer.

Still, it's hard to think of summer today when the weather has switched from beautiful this morning by the pool in the rocks to winter-ish this afternoon on Glenmill's main street. ("That's Scotland for you," Mr Fraser joked when he set off in his van with Cam and his busted bike, after temporarily fixing the gates.)

"Yeah, super cute," says Weezy, pulling her parka more tightly around her. "Cute as a kitten. Cute as a *box* of kittens. Now can we ditch the village tour and get that hot chocolate?"

To celebrate RJ coming home, we're eating cake – and hot chocolate – out.

We're also celebrating the fact that the paparazzi bloke wasn't there (Mr Fraser and Cam went to look for him and only found a few empty Coke cans from when he must've staked out the house). He shouldn't be back either, not now the gates are closed and RJ's called and got his lawyers on to the case.

"Sure," RJ answers Weezy. "Is that it there?"

RJ points to the only commercial building in a street full of mismatching houses. Its lights are like beams of comfort in the late afternoon chilly gloom.

"Yes, but don't get too excited. Remember, it's not got the most fancy menu," Mum laughs, as we begin to hurry towards the Cairn Café.

"It's fine as long as you like Tunnock's Teacakes," I manage to almost joke. I'm actually dying to see what world-touring RJ makes of the corny tartan interior of the café and the even cornier background music on offer.

"Wow, it looks busy," says Mum as we approach the steamed-up windows and see the dark outlines of figures inside.

With a tinkle of the old-fashioned bell above the door, we're in – and me and RJ slide into the one free table by the window.

"Just going to find the loo," says Weezy, leaving us to wend her way through the tables busy with walkers and little old ladies, mostly.

"Oh, look," says Mum as she shrugs off her jacket and hangs it on the back of a chair. "There's Cam, and that must be his mum. I'll just pop over and say hi..."

Sure enough, Cam waves over in our direction, and I shyly wave back at him. A dog – either Joe or Bella – rests its head on the table, its nostrils sniffing hopefully at the newly arrived food on the plates there.

"*He* seems nice," says RJ, and I turn to see dimples in his cheeks that I've never noticed before. I'm being teased.

"Cam's ... OK, I suppose. I don't really know him very well," I reply, feeling redness heat my cheeks. "He spoke a lot to Weezy this morning, when we met him at the pool. She might have more of an opinion of him than I do."

"Oh, my Weezy has an opinion on *everyone*, and isn't afraid to let people know," laughs RJ. "This afternoon, when we had our chat, she really ripped into me. Told me in no uncertain terms why I'd let her down the last few years. I probably deserved it. And Weezy deserved to be allowed to rant at me. Though at least she told me she loved me at the end of it all."

I'd vaguely heard the boom of their voices from my room, as they thrashed out their differences in the old nursery, just across the landing in the main house.

But I don't respond to what RJ just said. One, because I'm jealous that Weezy has a dad she can rant at in close quarters. And two, because I know she has an opinion of *me*. (And it's not a good one.) RJ notices my sudden silence.

"Hey, how have *you* been getting on with my Weezy-Woo?" he asks.

"Er ... well..." I mumble, not knowing what to make of that cutesy nickname for such a brittle girl, OR what to say about our stunning lack of stepsisterly bonding so far.

"Uh-oh, not so good?" RJ suggests.

I come out with a nervous sort of laugh in reply.

"Don't let Weezy's hard shell fool you," RJ says conspiratorially, glancing over to the door of the *Lassies* loos in the Cairn Café. "She's a softie underneath. It's just that she's had a tough time of it lately. Her mum's not an easy person to live with; *I'm* always touring and not around for her; and she's pretty much on course to fail all her exams because of both of us messing her up. And then her dyslexia doesn't help, of course."

Oh. I instantly think of Weezy's finger tracing

along the board at the Linn o' Glenmill this morning. So that *wasn't* just a casual gesture; it's what she physically needed to do to help her read the information. . . ? The kind part of me feels a little sorry and sweeter towards her.

"If you could just be a bit patient with Weezy, that would be great," RJ implores me with a winning smile. "All of this is so new and hard for her to get used to."

RJ waves his hand around. It could be that he's referring to the dubious delights of the Cairn Café, but obviously, he's talking about Wilderwood, Mum and me. The *less* kind part of me feels grumpy that RJ hasn't noticed that "all of this" is pretty new and hard for me too. I feel a sudden need to get away from RJ's pep talk.

"Back in a minute," I tell him, and get to my feet.

He surprises me by grabbing hold of my hand before I go.

"Hey, I also wanted to say sorry to you, Ellis," he says.

"What for?" I ask, awkwardness curdling in my stomach.

("Sorry, but I'm thinking about sending you off to boarding school, same as Weezy"?)

"Sorry for everything being such a whirlwind," says RJ. "I know me getting together with your mum happened like *that* –" he snaps the fingers of his free hand "– and it's been kind of hard on you. Not to mention moving here. You've got to remember, your mum and me, we're older – well, *I'm* a lot older. And suddenly, when things seem right, you just think, hey, life's too short – let's go for it!"

I blink down at RJ, wanting his words to be genuine, but not totally sure if they are.

"The thing is, being away from you guys," he continues, "I got a bit of perspective. And maybe I was a bit selfish, and didn't think of the impact on you when I scooped your gorgeous mother off to be my bride. So I'm sorry, Ellis. Truly."

OK, so RJ sounds like he means it. Truly. Maybe I was overreacting and there *are* no plans for boarding schools. But then once he's back here for good, will RJ and Mum roll themselves up in that bubble of love and leave me out anyway?

I don't think I know my stepdad well enough to ask that (or even *think* of him as my stepdad), so instead I just mumble a shy "That's OK" and set off towards the loos.

My cheeks are hot and I'm feeling flustered,

partly because of what RJ's been saying and partly because I'm aware Cam's staring. As my mum and his chat, I sense his blackbird eyes locked on me as I weave my way between the tables, past the TV and video player featuring the man singing his jolly songs, accompanied by his noisy accordion.

I manage to mutter a mumbled hello Cam's way (and a pat of a random dog's head) as I reach the far wall ... where I almost walk straight into Weezy. She must've come out of the loo, but has stopped on her way back to us, her attention grabbed by a particular framed photo on the wall. The one of the stiff and stern family and staff of Wilderwood Hall.

"It's – it's a great picture, isn't it?" I say, knowing that RJ will be watching, hoping me and his Weezy-Woo will be getting on.

Well, I'm trying, but at the same time I'm fixing my gaze, of course, on one face in particular. What's happening in Flora's world right now? I wonder. Will she be getting snapped at by another member of staff for some made-up misdemeanour, or will the servants all be too busy, getting in a tizzy of preparation for the trip to London and beyond?

When we get back home to Wilderwood, I'll try to slip away – slip *back* – and find her. . .

"All these people," murmurs Weezy, intrigued by the photo, if not me. "You just wish you could know all about their lives, don't you? For instance, *this* girl. She looks so sad. What do you think her life was like?"

My heart thuds in my chest at the coincidence of Weezy's finger landing on Flora.

"I – I'm not sure," I say, flustered, turning to face Weezy.

And then everything. . . everything begins to sink sideways and downwards and dark.

(Whirl, tilt, shift.)

17

"I'm absolutely fine," I insist for the millionth time.

"She's not been eating enough," says Mum to anyone who'll listen, which is me, RJ and Weezy. All four of us are in the small, temporary living room of the East Wing. "You know, I think I'll get her something else. . ."

Mum pushes herself up from the sofa and heads to the kitchen for some more of the vat of bolognese she made everyone for tea.

"I really don't need—" I begin to protest, and then realize I'm wasting my time.

Mum won't take no for an answer, even though I've proved I'm OK now and already had a bowl of her bolognese and garlic bread too.

"*Sure* you're OK, lovely Miss Harper?" asks RJ, stopping softly strumming his guitar to lean over and pat my leg. "Or do you want everyone to stop asking?"

I appreciate the jokey remark and smile gratefully at him. Obviously, I'd quite like to forget that I sort-of-but-not-quite fainted in front of a packed café, and managed to fall backwards on to Cam, but not before I'd tried to break my fall by putting my hand on his mum's slice of carrot cake and squashing it flat.

That same (now clean) hand is currently in Weezy's lap. I don't know if she thinks offering to paint my nails navy blue is in some way medicinal, or will at least maybe help take my mind off what happened in the café, but whichever, I appreciate it. And the colour's pretty great too.

My other hand is done already. While Weezy concentrated on stroking polish carefully on to each nail, I kept sneaking a peek at her, searching for that fierce look of hers ... but it didn't seem to be there any more.

Isn't it funny? Earlier today, when I'd been at the side of the building with Flora, I was flooded with loneliness. But now – with RJ strumming away and

Weezy all softened and painting my nails – I can't help but feel a small, delicate sense of *happy*. The sort of thing that you don't want to think about too much in case it gets shy and twitchy and vanishes on you. . .

Actually, the first flutter of happiness started up on the car journey back to Wilderwood, when Mrs Fraser insisted on driving Mum and me home while RJ and Weezy tramped back via the shortcut through the field. It was too hard to hang on to my embarrassment when both Cam's sheepdogs kept trying to lick me to death, with Cam doing these stupid cartoon voices for each of them. ("Who *is* this?" "I dunno, but I like her. I wonder what her nose tastes of?" "Ooh, can I lick it first? Can I, can I?")

Even with something simple like Mum fussing over me once we got dropped off, settling me on the sofa, putting my feet up, getting me a cloth for my forehead and a glass of iced water, the flutters of happiness kept coming.

And they kept fluttering all the more when RJ brought his acoustic guitar in from the hire car, sat himself down in one of the squashy white armchairs and began to gently pick out the notes of something new he was working on. ("Haven't got any lyrics yet; it's just something I'm playing around with.")

But hiding behind the flutters are those familiar ripples, lurking, biding their time, ready to roll in.

The trouble is, I'm just not sure it's safe to feel good. I'm not sure I can trust that it's OK to.

"Look, I'll go speak to your mum and try to stop her from force-feeding you," says RJ, putting the guitar down and pushing himself up off the chair. "Back in a sec. . ."

"No, you don't have to," I mumble, but he's gone.

And now I'm alone with Weezy. What are we supposed to say to each other? Do I come right out and ask her why she's doing something vaguely nice for me all of a sudden?

"That was pretty wild, what happened back there," says Weezy, without looking up at me.

So *that's* it. In movies, people don't like each other, but then when something over-the-top scary happens to one of them, the other realizes life's too short (like RJ said back in the café) and they make up, etc., etc. Well, this isn't a movie, and nothing over-the-top scary happened to me. I went a bit light-headed in an old-fashioned café, that's all, as far as anyone is concerned (even if *I* know differently).

But it was obviously enough to rattle Weezy. And if she feels sorry for me, that's fine, especially if it means she stops shooting me the evils and carries on painting my nails this great colour.

"What did *you* feel?" Weezy asks, now lifting her brown eyes to meet mine.

"I – I just. . ."

Stumbling over my words, I grind to a halt. I'd been about to describe the sense of swirling and sinking when my mind properly registered what Weezy just said. The way she put the emphasis on "*you*". "What did *you* feel?" It meant *she* felt something too. . .!

"Dizzy. I just felt dizzy," I say eventually, blinking back at her.

"Look, don't freak out or anything," says Weezy, holding the nail polish brush in mid-air. "But just that second when we looked at each other, the weirdest thing happened. It was like I saw a – a – shadow coming over you."

I jerk as a blob of navy-blue varnish drops unexpectedly on to my thumb. And whatever Weezy said, I *am* freaking out. I don't understand what she saw, but it feels like she was *almost* able to peek into my other world, my other Wilderwood.

And that can't happen.

It's mine, mine and Flora's.

"Got to get a drink of water," I mutter, slipping my hand off Weezy's lap and getting up to leave the softly lit room and this staring girl.

I suddenly, urgently want to keep the two parts of my life separate, so the tiny, fluorescent-lit kitchen and the comfort of my smiling, chatty mum is all I want right now.

Except Mum seems a bit busy at the moment, I see, when I hover in the kitchen doorway. She's over by the chipped worktop, having some earnest conversation with RJ. An earnest, *secret* conversation, it seems, since they jump apart guiltily when they notice me.

"Hey, gorgeous!" say Mum, switching her smile on and holding out her arms to me.

I don't go straight to her. Instead, I warily prop myself against the fridge. Mum and RJ exchange fleeting glances. And those secret looks; they send the last few of my happiness butterflies reeling off into the dark corners of this huge, echoing house.

"Better get back to my guitar ... that song won't write itself, will it?" RJ jokes, reaching out to ruffle my hair as he leaves us.

"Are you all right, Ellis?" asks Mum. "Not feeling rubbish again, are you?"

What's really rubbish is knowing you're being talked about. What's really rubbish is secrets.

I picture my phone, lying dropped somewhere in the mess of my unpacking, and remind myself that I was brave enough to hang up on Shaniya. To delete her from my contacts and my life.

I can be brave like that again. I can ask my mum straight out. 'Cause after all, isn't it better to be angry on the outside (like Weezy) than scared on the inside (like me)?

"What's going on?" I ask as I start to pick at my barely dry navy nails. "Why are you and RJ talking about me?"

"Oh, but we weren't," Mum says hurriedly and unconvincingly. "We were chatting about ... house stuff."

Body language. Mum's nibbling at the inside of her mouth. She's lying; keeping something from me for sure. And then I think of a trick I heard that counsellors and therapists do; they go totally quiet, which *forces* their patients to say more.

So I fix Mum with a long look, and wait. It works.

"OK, OK . . . we were just talking about these – these turns of yours," she says at last. "We think they may be some kind of panic attack."

"I know, I heard RJ say so on the phone, when we were driving back from the pool this morning."

Mum is taken aback.

"You heard? Sorry, Ellis – you weren't meant to. I thought you were listening to your music," she says apologetically. "But anyway, they keep happening, don't they? And they're worse than your usual waves. . ."

The "turns" Mum is talking about; I know they're not panic attacks. But whatever they are all of them, I realize now with shock and sureness, have been somehow linked to my connection to Flora, and to both my Wilderwoods. For a split second, I wonder if I should come clean and tell her that, tell Mum *everything*, but my mind is so muddled and I'm so very angry with her that the words won't come.

"Mmm," I mumble instead, wondering where she's going with this.

"So, I'm thinking that I should make an appointment with the local doctor for you," she says, tilting her head, as if she's waiting for me to flip out. I don't.

To be honest, I'm flooded with a sudden sense of relief. I mean, I know no doctor can help with the whirls, tilts and shifts, but I am *so* tired of the never-ending waves that ripple and roll and ruin everything. My shoulders sink and tears prickle in my eyes.

"Aw, Ellis, baby! C'mere," says Mum, spotting what's happening and opening her arms to me again. This time I go over, and sink gratefully into her small-but-strong hug, resting my tired head on her shoulder.

"I know it all started at your last school, because of not settling and the friendship issues and everything," Mum mutters softly in my ear. "And that's one of the reasons I thought coming here would do you good. A fresh start."

Oh... This whole move – it wasn't *just* about Mum and RJ and their Shiny New Project? She was thinking about me too in all this?

"But you know, maybe I was a bit naïve to think the anxiety would switch off, like a light, the moment we got here," she carries on with her soothing voice and that comforting circular stroke of my back. "I just think we might need a little help to send it on its way. Don't you? Especially if you're starting at a new school."

"Maybe," I murmur in reply, into the softness of her pink Arran jumper. I might tower over Mum when I'm standing, but right now I feel as cosy and held and safe as the tiniest of toddlers.

And that feeling lasts for, ooh ... all of three seconds. Because I've suddenly noticed something over Mum's shoulder. Some random bits of paper plopped on the work surface. Scribbled to-do notes for Mr Fraser. Something that looks like a paint colour chart. A brochure.

It's the brochure that makes my heart stumble and practically stop. Tucked – possibly hastily – at the bottom of the pile, the heading on it is still mostly visible. Enough that I know it says INVERKELLEN SCHOOL.

OK, so it's *not* a brochure; it's a prospectus. A prospectus for the boarding school Mum and RJ must be considering for me, as soon as the local doctor "sorts me out".

"Ellis?" says Mum as I pull myself free from her.

"It's fine. I'm fine," I say flatly. "Think I'll just go lie down in my room."

Wow. There's a great big secret right here in the kitchen, and Mum's *still* not able to come out with it. So all this time, I've been fooling myself about how close we really are. What a joke...

An overwhelming feeling of loneliness wells up inside me, making me feel almost sick, and all I want to do is run from it and the waves. But I don't want Mum to see me cry, so with all the calm I can fake, I walk steadily out of the kitchen, down the corridor and into my room.

Pressing the door closed behind me, I slide down it on to the floor with my back against it so no one can come in. Because right now, I want to see no one but Flora. Only Flora keeps the waves at bay. I close my eyes tight, press my hands palm down on the cool floorboards, and will the whispers to come...

18

At first there's nothing.

All I'm aware of is the sky beyond the two windows, a sunset glow, a mesmerizing meld of mauve and tangerine over the now black-green Scottish hills and pines.

"Please come," I say softly, pressing my hands harder into the floor, stretching my fingers so wide they start to prickle with pins and needles.

Only it's not pins and needles, is it?

"*Turn . . . turn . . . turn. . .*"

As well as the whisperings, I hear a faint crackle.

"*Turn the corner, I'll be there!*"

My eyes flip open and I see Flora kneeling by the

grate, singing as she brushes coal dust from around the busily burning evening fire.

"That's a pretty tune," says Miss Matilda. She's sitting at a writing desk by the two small windows of my room (*her* room!).

"Thank you, miss. A dear friend taught it to me," says Flora, and I see her smiling to herself.

"Someone from back in your home village?" Miss Matilda doesn't look up from her writing as she chats.

"No, someone local. *Very* local," says Flora, then turns her head from her work and gives me a wink. I stifle a giggle, even though Miss Matilda wouldn't be able to hear it. It's so good to giggle; it's so good to see Flora. When she finishes here, I'll follow her out, and tell her my news. She'll be busy, of course, but I'll follow her while she works her way around the rooms, lighting fires before everyone heads for bed.

"How nice. Is it a young man?" Miss Matilda asks Flora.

"Oh, no, miss. Can't be doing with one of them," says my friend, straightening up and wiping her hands on a cloth rag she has draped over her shoulder.

"I'm very glad to hear it! By the way —"

At this point Miss Matilda puts her pen down and swivels elegantly around in her chair to face Flora. I can see now that she's wearing a long fitted robe that looks like a cross between a dressing gown and a coat. A perfect night-time fashion to suit a cold, draughty Scottish mansion, I suppose.

"– I heard from Catriona that you are to stay behind when we leave for the trip next week. I'm sorry to hear that. You must be very disappointed."

Miss Matilda doesn't seem to be looking down her nose at Flora at all. Just as I thought, she seems quite kind and fair.

"A little," says Flora, her head bent shyly.

"And you are to clean the house from top to bottom while we're away? That does sound a rather big job to undertake," says Miss Matilda, frowning noticeably, as if she is well aware of the injustice of Flora's situation.

"The under-butler is to stay too, miss, and Mrs Strachan has already hired an older lady experienced in laundry and basic cooking," Flora explains.

"Still, Wilderwood is a large house to maintain," says Miss Matilda, tilting her head sympathetically.

That simple, small tilt gives me sudden hope for Flora. A governess has some social standing in a household like this. Once the family returns from America, perhaps Miss Matilda will be an ally for Flora. And if the rest of the staff see that Miss Matilda has a good opinion of her, then perhaps things can change. . .

"I was thinking of saying so to Mrs Strachan," Flora says, sounding suddenly excited. "And I thought I might tell her that I know of a girl who could help me."

Another surge of hope lifts my spirits. It would be so lovely for Flora to have company in the huge, empty rooms of Wilderwood.

"And who would that be?" asks Miss Matilda.

I see a smile playing at the corner of Flora's lips, but she's smart enough to control it so she doesn't seem as if she's cheeking the governess.

"You know I mentioned my dear friend?" says Flora.

A faint sense of uncertainty causes me to stiffen.

"The person who taught you that song?" Miss Matilda asks as she gets up and walks closer to Flora and the mantelshelf, where she checks her hair in the mirror above it. Now she's closer I can smell her sweet, flowery perfume.

"Yes, that same person," says Flora, shooting me a

sideways look of glee. "She is only thirteen, but she's very tall and strong. And she has no family. Well, none that care for her the way they should."

A hot flush is rising through my entire body. What is Flora suggesting? That I shift permanently into her world? And I absolutely *don't* want to leave behind my version of Wilderwood, however difficult it's been so far.

"My, that sounds like a very sensible plan," says Miss Matilda, taking some pins from her hair and letting her thick, long braid fall loose down her back. "I certainly think you should speak to Mrs Strachan in the morning and she can perhaps find money in her household budget. A girl that young should not cost too much to hire, surely."

"Yes, miss. Thank you for your advice, miss," says Flora, beaming and bobbing as she picks up her scuttle to leave. Her face is a picture of happiness. When she looks away from Miss Matilda and catches sight of *my* expression, she'll see that it's not a mirror image.

"Uh . . . just one thing before you go, Flora," says Miss Matilda, now frowning as she looks down at the mantelshelf. "I put my cameo brooch down here few minutes ago. Have you seen it?"

"No, miss," Flora says, suddenly pinking. Even with the fire crackling and burning, a chill cuts through the air.

"Are you sure?"

"No, I mean, yes, I'm sure, miss," says Flora, now clearly ruffled and upset. Miss Matilda turns around to face her full on, the warmth gone from her.

"Flora, I have always given you the benefit of the doubt, when others did not. And I will give you the benefit of the doubt once again," she says with ice in her voice. "If my brooch happens to be here in the morning, after you have cleaned my room, I will say no more. But if it is not, I shall have to report the matter to Mrs Strachan."

"It's not fair, I have not seen it!" says Flora, getting agitated and tearful.

"That is my final word. Goodnight, Flora," says Miss Matilda, moving towards the door.

I slip to the side as the governess pulls it open, and then follow Flora out into the corridor. The door is closed firmly shut after us.

"Come, come," Flora says hurriedly, looking this way and that down the corridor, before pulling me into the privacy of her and Minnie's room, which seems even more drab and awful than ever.

"Do you see what it is like for me here, Ellis?" Flora whispers, forcing the tears from her face with the heels of her hands. "But as you say, I should look forward to them all being gone. And won't we have such a fine time together?" She gives me a watery, hopeful smile, which I struggle to return.

Because for the first time in *this* Wilderwood, the waves come rolling in, thick and fast.

"Flora, I can't just leave my family for ever!" I tell her.

"But you said your mother only had eyes for her new husband. You said they were to send you away anyway!" Flora protests.

"Yes, I did say that but – but—"

But even if it *is* true about Inverkellen – and I know it is, since I've seen the proof – I am braver than I used to be. Like I boasted to Flora in the housemaid's closet, I can say no. I *will* say no. I'll agree to seeing the doctor and I'll do my best at Glenmill High, and Mum and RJ will have to be happy with that.

"And you have no friends where you are, do you?" Flora carries on with her objections, desperate for me to see sense. *Her* sense.

But at her words, I picture myself at the pool in

the rocks. Cam bobbing in the water, aiming his smile at me, Bella and Joe paddling and panting around him. And I imagine what it would be like to join in with his fun; to answer his three word challenge, instead of clamming up and letting Weezy do the talking.

And Weezy; what would it be like to have more moments like the one we had on the sofa just now? An older sister painting her younger sister's nails. Talking about teenager stuff together...

"I – I just can't come and live with you, Flora, I'm so sorry," I tell her.

Maybe I'm expecting my friend's face to fall, tears of disappointment to drip-drop down her sallow cheeks. What I *don't* expect is the pure rage that's visible in her clenched jaw and the sharp slap to my face. The stinging pain of it makes my eyes shut tight.

When I open them again, only a stunned moment later, it's a different set of brown eyes that happens to be staring into mine. In a very different Wilderwood, I'm so thankful to see.

"Is it OK if I come in?" Weezy asks, standing at the doorway of the "guest" bedroom she rejected.

"Uh-huh," I mumble, at the same time flopping

down on to the floor into a sitting position. I'm shaking so much that I can't stand for a second more.

"Do you feel bad again?" Weezy asks. "Should I get your mum?"

"No . . . and no," I say. "I'll be fine. I'm just the tiniest bit dizzy."

"Well, lie flat then, if you don't mind the dust."

Weezy's voice gets closer to me, and I see she's now crouching down beside me.

"Actually, put your head here," she orders me.

She's kneeling down, patting her thighs. Warily, I do as I'm told and lie back, using her lap as a pillow. I can't say it's relaxing though. After what just happened with Flora, I can't imagine ever relaxing again. And then Weezy starts drawing loops with her fingertips through my hair and across my forehead.

"Is this pressure OK?" she asks.

"Yes," I mutter shyly. "It feels . . . pretty nice."

"Oh, good!" she laughs lightly. "I don't know what I'm doing really, but it's supposed to be an Indian Head Massage. The nurse at my old school used to give me one whenever I got these stress headaches. Which was almost always. Ha!"

"Did you have a hard time there?" I ask her.

"Hard? Being surrounded by A-star students, when I'm struggling to even read what the homework assignment is supposed to be? Yep, I've had a hard time there," Weezy says firmly. "Plus me and my flowery DMs never fitted in with the other girls, really."

"Why did RJ make you go there, if you were so unhappy?" I ask, niggles of doubts about my "friendly" stepfather creeping in again.

"Oh, it wasn't *his* idea. It was my mum's. She was determined I went to 'the best school possible', even if it wasn't the best school possible for *me*. Over and over again, Dad tried to tell her it wasn't working, but Mum wouldn't have it. She told him that he was away so much touring that he had no right to an opinion on the matter." Weezy's words drift over me as her fingers magically make the waves melt away.

"Does your mother actually hate RJ?" I ask her, letting my eyes slowly shut.

"Only enough to try to turn me against him," Weezy replies wearily . "Which worked, a lot of the time. *And* to keep his letters and even his *wedding* secret from me."

Hate seems so harsh. I feel a pang for my mum,

who's tried very hard not to say a bad word to me about my disappearing dad and my disappointing granny all these years, even though they both definitely deserve it. But there is one thing, rather than person, that I hate.

"I hate secrets," I mumble.

"Wow, *that* sounded bitter," Weezy laughs wryly. "Who's keeping secrets from you?"

"My mum," I answer.

"Oh. . ."

She knows. She *knows*!

I flip my eyes open and roll off Weezy's lap, curling myself up on the musty, cold floor, facing away from her.

"So when's she planning on sending me to Inverkellen?" I demand, my heart pounding.

"What?" says Weezy, sounding aghast. "It's not *you* going there, Ellis – it's me! Well, it's a possibility Sadie and Dad want me to think about, if I don't want to go back to my old school to do my A levels. The thing is, I don't want to do A levels at *all*, but if I have to, I'd rather just go right here in the village, to Glenmill High. . ."

I stare blindly along the faded floorboards at the dirt-edged skirting board, my head throbbing with confusion. Weezy might be staying here, and starting at the same school as me? So Mum wasn't keeping secrets after all. . . ?

"Anyway, if we're talking secrets, here's one of mine," I hear Weezy say, and feel her hand land lightly on my shoulder. "I can be a jealous idiot. I was madly jealous of your mum, till I arrived here and got to know her and realized how amazing and lovely she is. And I was madly jealous of you especially."

"Me?" I whisper, not moving from the comfort of my curled-up pose. "Why me?"

"Because look how similar we are, with our height and everything! You remind me of *me*, only younger. And you're getting to spend time with my dad. I mean, it nearly *killed* me when I saw him run and pick you up earlier."

"So what changed?" I say softly.

"Dad told me stuff about you this afternoon, about the hassles at your old school and your – your. . ."

"Anxiety issues," I fill in for her, so she doesn't have to feel like she's saying something clunky and insensitive.

"Yeah, *that*. Anyway, after our talk, it just got me thinking that me and you don't just have being tall in common. We've both gone through similar emotional stuff, for our own reasons," says Weezy. "So I realized you were OK. And, hey, probably... well, probably just as amazing and lovely as your mum."

A pleased smile sneaks on to my lips. But then I realize there's a hole in our conversation. A hole where a secret is hidden.

'Cause just now, when I spoke about Mum having a secret, Weezy said a knowing "Oh..."

If the secret wasn't about me going to boarding school, then what is it? At least I know Weezy is taking a chance on liking me now. Which means there's a good chance of her answering my question. I go to speak, but the first thing that pops out of my mouth is a startled "Ow!!"

Painful sparks are spiking my fingertips, where they're resting on the floorboards.

"*Mine... Mine... Mine...*"

The whispers rise from the wood. And my heart plummets with pure dread.

19

This can't be happening. I'm still in my own Wilderwood – I can feel Weezy's hand resting on my shoulder. But I'm halfway inside the *other* Wilderwood too, suddenly staring under a bed, candlelight casting long shadows.

A faded, well-worn, hand-crocheted blanket covers rough grey blankets, which are tucked into the space between the mattress and broken-looking springs. And just out of reach, I spot some kind of bundle that's been shoved underneath the bed. It looks like it's made of a cleaning rag – the sort that's kept in the housemaid's closet. Nothing I see here looks beautiful or sweet, but still, something *smells* sweet. A powdery soft whiff of scent I can't place.

I wriggle, trying to sit up, but find I can't move properly – I'm somehow pinned here by the deepening weight of Weezy's hand. All I can do is try lengthening my arm, just that little stretch further, and yes ... I've managed to gather a piece of the fabric in my fingertips and gingerly pull it towards me.

"That's mine," says a voice close to my ear. My eyes meet Flora's. She's crouched down, wearing a nightgown and shawl, her feet bare. She's frantically trying to grab the small bundle from me, but I hold as tight as I'm able to.

My grip isn't firm enough, though, and she finally manages to tug and snatch it from me. But with that sudden snatch, the bundle unravels ... and a flurry of objects spills out. Coins, an earring, a pocket watch, a silver spoon, a St Christopher medallion, some blocky object I can't make out – it's dark in here, with only a candle for light – and then rumbling and rolling clumsily across the floor is an oval brooch. A cameo. A piece of jewellery that has the flowery scent of its owner clinging gently to it.

Her breathing sounding panicked, Flora quickly gathers up her treasures while I lie trapped between two worlds, watching. And as she grabs the last object, I recognize it with a jolt; it seems I'm not the *only* one who's dipped in between worlds. Flora has found and saved my broken, dead phone from the floor of my room – brushed off my windowsill and forgotten – even though she can have no clue what it is or what it could do. . .

A harsh coughing startles me, and Flora too. She jumps up and the air is stirred. Spiralling columns of smoke begin to wind down towards the floorboards.

"Flora – what's happening!" shrieks a frightened voice, between coughs. A figure struggles to wake up and sit up in the other bed.

"It's a fire, Minnie," says Flora, her voice retreating as she leaves the room.

"But what do I do?"

"Run, you fool!" Flora's voice drifts back.

As Minnie's bare feet stamp past me I can hear the sounds of more hysteria in the house. Shouts and screams, names being yelled. But it's the urgent call for help that cuts through to the core of me. I wriggle free of the statue-still hand of Weezy, and scramble to my feet.

Like the haze of a not-quite-there rainbow, the image of my stepsister hovers hazily in the middle of the floor. But everything in this *older* Wilderwood is pin-sharp, especially that voice.

"Help me! Please, someone!"

Out in the corridor, I come face-to-face with the door to my room. Fire is licking up it, smoke billowing as the toxic paint pops and blisters. The top half of the door shakes as Miss Matilda, trapped inside, hammers her fists desperately against it.

"Help! It's locked!" I hear her call out again, her words punctuated with coughs and gasps.

I feverishly glance around at the floor, searching for a key to the lock that – I realize with a jolt – is not there in my time. But all I see are bundled-up sections of a newspaper, which must have been used to deliberately set the small blaze.

A tiny scrap of one flutters in the updraught, edges alight. Printed on it is the single bold letter from a newspaper title, and partial date: *April 1912* ... and then it flitters and burns to a blackened ember in mid-air.

I fight a punch of panic. I'm from the future Wilderwood, I remind myself, so nothing in *this* world can happen to me! That means I need to stay calm and find a way to help Miss Matilda. I pull open the connecting door to the main house, looking around for anything that might help me smash open the door of my bedroom. Glancing along the landing, I see the master and the mistress being ushered down the grand stairway by a footman. Then my gaze lands on a vase on a stand close by. The vase ... the stand; would either of those work?

Probably not; they're both too fine and frail and would just smash to a pile of china or firewood at the first impact.

"Mamma! Papa!" cries the little boy, being carried quickly out of the bedroom next to the nursery in the arms of Catriona.

The nursery ... it's directly in front of me. Maybe there's something in there? I stand in the doorway, gazing at useless toys, rocking horses and clutter. And the clutter includes – I realize with a start – a futon mattress on the floor with bedding piled on top and Weezy's hoodie flung across it. Which means that *if* I'm dipping between the old and new Wilderwoods, some of Mr Fraser's tools could be in here too... I kick aside teddies and push-along dogs – and nearly cry with relief when I see it: a paint-splattered vinyl bag of shiny tools. I rummage, find a hammer, and hurry back to destroy my bedroom door.

Behind it now comes the sound of coughing and sobbing.

"I'll get you out!" I yell, though Miss Matilda can't hear me.

Thankfully, she *can* hear the sharp bangs as I thwack repeatedly at the brass lock and doorknob.

"Oh, mercy!" she calls from inside. "Hurry, please – I can't breathe!"

I use all my strength for the last, splintering crack as the locking mechanism breaks off, and then a rush of energy barges into and straight through me. It's a man – I vaguely recognize him from the print in the Cairn Café. He was in his full butler's uniform then, rather than just a flapping shirt and hastily pulled-on trousers with dangling braces, as he's dressed now. But Miss Matilda is in no shape to be surprised at Mr Stewart's disarray; as soon as he pushes the door open she falls gratefully into his arms.

Watching him run off with her towards the back stairs and safety, I step slowly through the fire and the smoke towards the window. I peer out, down on to a scene of total confusion in the garden below; people are crying and comforting each other, some holding lamps to help the strongest men see so they can pump water from a large barrel on wheels into waiting buckets. Some are even using jugs and teapots to scoop water from the fountain and throw it uselessly in the direction of the building.

Only one person is on her own, standing still, staring up. Despite the heat, I feel a fierce chill inside when we lock eyes. Because Flora did this. Flora risked the life of the governess. She did it because she was raging at *me*, and worried Miss Matilda had found her out as a thief and would tell.

As I look down at her clutching her bundle of stolen treasures, I can't believe someone I cared for could be so calculating and cruel... But then Flora was obviously an expert at secrets; only her secrets were the wrong kind, the lying kind.

The only thing true about Flora, I see now – with a churn of the stomach – was that she did everything everyone accused her of. Of *course* she deliberately scalded Minnie with hot water. Of *course* she encouraged little Archibald to scorch his expensive toy. The dead mouse in Jean's bed; tricks and meannesses like that and more made Flora glad and made her sing inside. And when I came upon her in the grand bathroom, I see with a keener eye now what she was up to . . . she wasn't sniffing Mrs Richards' perfume bottle at all. She was spitting in it.

Oh, that poor dog with the rat poison. . .

But Flora's tortured expression tells me something else that is true. She knows this time she went too far. And I think *I've* gone too far. Too far from my time and place.

I turn and run back through the flames and smoke I cannot feel, past the young men now thundering towards me with their buckets of water and handkerchiefs tied around their faces, and allow myself to fall towards the bare floorboards of Flora and Minnie's room. As I fall, I can only hope that someone will be there to catch me. . .

At the last micro-second I feel her pull me to her, and let out a long slow breath as Weezy's arms cradle me close.

"It's OK, Ellis!" she's saying, unaware of where I've just been and what I've just seen. "I've got you, don't cry!"

But I *do* cry, with sheer relief at being here in this world, with this girl and not the other. . .

Time is a funny thing. It sounds so rigid, if you talk about it in maths speak, doesn't it? Sixty seconds in a minute. Fourteen days in a fortnight. Three hundred and sixty-six days in a leap year.

But we all know it's much bendier and stretchier than that. Even a number-loving maths professor knows that time goes fast when you're having fun and drags when you're bored.

For me, the last five months have passed in a blur of spring and summer, plaster dust and cold dips in the pool in the rocks. As for this last week, it's whizzed by in about five minutes, with me and Mum speeding around London, catching up with all sorts of people and places. And now I can't believe it's the last day of the holidays, and school starts back tomorrow. . .

Ting-a-ling-a-ling!

Stepping into the Cairn Café, I'm immediately glad all over again that the new owners decided to keep the chirpy bell above the door, even if they didn't keep much else – apart from a stock of Tunnock's Teacakes. 'Cause yes, they ditched the tartan plastic and the dusty thistles. They ditched the old TV and video machine, and so the hairy kilted man plays his accordion badly no more. They even ditched Moira. Or at least, she'd enjoyed her rest so much when her son and daughter-in-law shut for the place for renovations back in May that she decided to retire and be a customer and eat cake instead.

Another casualty of the makeover was the collection of black-and-white historical prints that used to hang on the walls, though they (mostly) were happily rehomed to people in the village. Moira specifically asked her son to set aside the Wilderwood Hall one for us, naturally. But one of the builders knocked that particular print off the wall, breaking the glass and scratching the photo so badly that he ended up chucking it in the skip and hoping no one would notice. Moira was *so* apologetic, and RJ and Mum were *kind* of disappointed, but to be honest, I was secretly relieved...

"Hey, look who it is!" yelps Weezy, almost clunking a full tray of food off some tourist's head when she spots me. "And spooky – how's that for timing?"

She points to the wall-mounted telly that's tuned to a music channel. Playing now is White Star Line's "Turn the Corner". I smile, but I don't love the coincidence ... not with the memories that particular track stirs up.

"Glad to see you back, baby sister!" Weezy calls out, and – after dumping down her order – comes racing over in her beloved Doc Martens and dip-dyed hair. (It's still red, just the ends are purple.)

Weezy's worked here since she got her A levels out of the way. She liked Glenmill High all right, but she's loving this job – and earning her own money – more, and is looking forward to doing a diploma course in hospitality in September.

And of course, Weezy's been a much more appropriate waitress for the new-look Cairn Café than Moira (bless her). That's because she matches the decor; the blown-up, high-definition photos on the walls are all of glorious Scottish redheads, with Weezy – the token *English* redhead – featuring in a prime spot by the loos.

That was Mum's design idea, of course. She's decided – as well as running the Hall as a location – to do a proper course in interior design once Wilderwood is finally finished. Though at the rate *that's* going, it'll be sometime in the next couple of decades. Not that we're in much of a hurry. Like I say, time's as strange and stretchy as a very long elastic band. . .

As Weezy squeezes the life out of me, Cam shouts over the tops of the heads of the tea-drinking, cake-eating walkers and tourists.

"Oi! I thought you weren't getting back till late tonight," he yelps.

He's at the table at the back. And now two little heads peer over the top of the table: sheepdogs Bella and Joe, who've sat up, all excited because their owner is excited, which is a pretty nice state of mind to be in at all times.

"We decided to come back from London a bit early, 'cause we were homesick," I say.

"I know who *you're* homesick for," Weezy teases me, nodding over in Cam's direction.

She knows me so well. With a quick kiss on the cheek just for her, I leave Weezy to get back to her waitressing and wriggle between the crowded tables to get to Cam.

"Well?" I say, beaming broadly at him.

He grins in return and pushes himself back in his chair. And there she is . . . curled up and fast asleep in his lap, her little legs twitching as she dreams her puppy dreams.

"Thanks for looking after her while we were away," I say to Cam, as I come around the table and dip down so I'm nose to nose with my best present ever.

"Yeah, it's been so tough," Cam jokes, pretending to wipe his brow.

Imagine . . . when we first came to Wilderwood, I stressed so much about the secret I thought Mum was keeping from me, and all the time it was about this little furry dollop of wonderfulness.

Yep, getting me a dog as soon as the Hall wasn't a death trap was what Mum and RJ were discussing in their phone calls and kitchen conversations. And when Mr Fraser told Mum that Bella was expecting a litter of pups, it was a no-brainer where we were going to find ourselves a dog.

"Minnie!" I whisper, and her ears twitch. "Hey, baby girl . . . I'm back."

She wakes up in a wibble-wobble of flying legs, licking tongue and yelping. My sweet Minnie... Of course, no one knows the *real* reason I called her that. Mum supposed it was after Minnie Mouse, and I'm more than happy to let her and everyone else believe that.

The truth is, I gave *my* Minnie the name when I first got her home, and let her explore the vast wonderland of Wilderwood. In the old kitchens downstairs, she ran out of energy, and flopped down by the cooking range. It was right where I'd first seen the poor put-upon kitchen maid through the crack in the door, being scalded with hot water by a certain housemaid. The name is cute, that's all. It's not as though I've ever slipped back into that time, that place since the day of the fire.

I don't know what changed exactly. Maybe it was just me suddenly feeling like I was home, finally.

Or maybe it was because Mr Fraser got the electrician to rip out every old, dangerous wire in the place as a top priority. ("Picture the headline: *RJ Johnstone's Love Nest Inferno!*" Weezy had joked at the time, not realizing how close to the truth that was, in the different version of Wilderwood at least...)

Whatever the reason, something was different; there was no buzzing or hissing or vibrations prickling in my fingertips. I've never heard whispering in the walls again either, and I'm glad.

Something *else* has changed too; I don't feel the big waves of anxiety the way I used to. They're small now, same as they are for every other average person, I like to think. Or at least, I'm getting there.

"Anyway, it's not just Minnie; *I'm* glad you're back too," says Cam, staring at me with those piercing eyes of his that always make me slightly unnerved. In a good way these days, though. "'Cause I've got something kind of insane to show you."

"Insane?" I repeat.

"Amazing, then," says Cam, handing me my puppy while he reaches down to grab his rucksack. "Come on, let's go..."

I'm not sure whether he's talking to me or Bella and Joe when he says that – but we all trot after him out of the café anyway.

A few seconds later, me and Cam are sitting – all three dogs at our feet – on the bench by the bus stop in the village high street.

"Ready?" asks Cam, reaching into his rucksack.

"I am preparing myself to be amazed," I joke.

And what Cam takes out looks like a bit of a joke too. What he's holding up in front of me is a very tatty copy of a local church magazine, dated 1972.

I glance up at Cam with a smile-and-frown mash-up.

"No, wait, this is worth it, promise," my best friend assures me, opening up the magazine and spreading it across our laps. The style of the mag is very home-made and old-fashioned, with tiny, dense type and no pictures on the page to brighten it up.

"So what's this about?" I ask as I try to stop Minnie biting her dad's tail, while at the same time reading a headline that says *International Disaster, Local Loss.*

"OK, so Mum came across a pile of these at the church jumble sale last Saturday. She was flicking through them, and then she saw *this* story. She said I had to show it to you."

I peer at the page, but it's hard to concentrate when a puppy is trying to scramble up on to your lap with surprisingly sharp claws.

"Can't you just tell me what it says, Cam?" I ask him while trying to calm Minnie.

"Sure . . . well, you know how you once wondered what happened to Wilderwood Hall, and why the original owners left it empty all those years ago?"

I nod. I may not have mentioned Flora to anyone, but I've spoken about the Hall plenty of times.

"According to this, Mr and Mrs Richards – and their staff – took a trip to America in 1912."

"Did they?" I say, though of course I already know that much.

"And listen to this bit, Ellis: *Unfortunately, this voyage of a lifetime ended in tragedy,*" Cam reads from the article. "*The ship they sailed on, operated by the White Star Line company, was none other than the infamous* Titanic. How about that?"

My breath leaves me, as if I've been punched – hard – in the chest.

"*Told* you it was insane!" says Cam.

Insane? I can't make sense of this; now ice-cold waves are rippling up my spine, giving me a case of brain freeze.

And then I get it.

The *Titanic*; that ship and what happened to it is the reason Wilderwood sat deserted for so many decades. The Richards family, all their staff, the reason they didn't come back because they *drowned*. It's too awful. It's too heartbreakingly sad.

Unless. . .

"Were there any survivors from that group? Does it say?" I ask Cam, clinging to hope for the likes of Miss Matilda, the little boy, poor scalded Minnie and the others.

"One," says Cam, peering at the tiny type. "A Mr Bill Stewart."

Stewart. The butler! The man who ran through me to rescue Miss Matilda.

But it seems he couldn't rescue her from the *Titanic*. . .

"Listen, there's more; someone *else* had a lucky escape," Cam continues. "It says here that there was a fire in the servants' quarters the week before the family left for their trip. The only person injured was the governess."

I hold myself tight, trying hard not to shiver.

"Apparently, smoke damaged her lungs, so she had to stay home – and survived, of course."

Relief rushes over me. I don't know what happened to Flora; whether she got found out and sacked, or stayed on as planned at Wilderwood, only to be sent away when the Richards never returned. Whatever her fate, I don't care. But at least Miss Matilda was spared a watery grave.

Suddenly, I just want to get home, to the Wilderwood that's in the here and now.

"Listen, I think I'd better get back and unpack," I tell Cam, getting up from the bench, even though the dogs would rather me and Minnie stayed and played.

"OK, but before you go," says Cam, standing up too, "I've got to tell you the best bit!"

He puts his hands on my shoulders and spins me round – and I find myself facing Honeysuckle Cottage, with its twists of peach and terracotta roses snaking all over the front of it.

"Guess who lived in this house in 1972?" Cam asks, but I can only shake my head. "Only the very, *very* old couple who were interviewed for this article. Bill and Matilda Stewart."

Bill and Matilda, I repeat in my head, trying to take this information in. Then I do my maths.

"The butler and governess from Wilderwood. . . ?" I mumble, hardly able to believe it, it's so amazing, just like Cam promised. "They got married!"

"Yep, they did. This article was written to

celebrate their sixtieth wedding anniversary," says Cam, looking back down at the magazine. "Here's a brilliant quote from Bill: *My Matilda felt particularly bad because one maid who wasn't supposed to go on the trip took her place. Matilda felt to blame for that poor lass's death. Well, that made me propose straight away. All that loss at sea – of the young maid and all the others of Wilderwood that we knew – it made me think we shouldn't waste a minute of our time together on this earth.*"

More shivers ripple up my spine.

The maid who died; it was Flora. The tight grip in the pit of my stomach tells me it's true.

"A happy ending, eh?" Cam says with a grin, enjoying the deliciousness of the story.

"A happy ending," I murmur, my head bursting with truths I can't share with my friend.

And here's one in particular: they do say good things can come from bad. Flora could've killed Miss Matilda in that fire, but in the end, by accident, she gave Miss Matilda her life – and true love. . .

21

Me and Minnie have come home via the shortcut through the field, since it's quicker, but anyway, the new gates and the intercom are such a faff. *Cam* likes them; or at least he likes looking at the video monitor whenever he comes here, and frightening visitors by growling at them through the speaker. Cam also likes the idea of the new studio in the stable block. Work still hasn't started on that yet, but Cam's made RJ promise he can be the tea boy for every future visiting band.

And now we're near the East Wing, I can hear music. It's the strum of a guitar, coming from the front of the building, from the terrace.

Minnie hears it too and darts towards the sound, pulling the lead right out of my hand.

I laugh and let her go, watching as she runs past the fountain that's now free of ivy. Mum started attacking it before we went to London, managing to pull away practically a century's worth of intertwined vines with a surprising amount of strength for someone so small and delicate. Today she's starting on the hard part, though, shovelling earth out of the basin section. She's determined to renovate the fountain and get it gushing water before the summer's over. Though there's no sign of Mum right now. . .

Except here she is, I see, as I round the corner of the building. She's taking a break, lounging on a deckchair next to RJ, wearing her gardening outfit of denim cut-offs, T-shirt and pink bandana.

Minnie's already found her, tail and bottom waggling madly as Mum rubs her ears.

"Hello!" says RJ, glancing up at me without pausing in his strumming. "How are you doing, Miss Johnstone?"

I smile at that. I *love* it that we went to court and that I'm now properly, officially a Johnstone – same as Mum, and RJ and Weezy. It makes me feel like

I'm part of a tribe, and that I'll never be the odd one out again. Same as it's kind of cool walking around with RJ and Weezy and being the smallest for once, by a few centimetres anyway.

"Yeah, I'm OK. It was good to catch up with Weezy and Cam. And get Minnie back, of course," I reply, my fingers tight around the magazine Cam gave me to keep. "By the way, that's sounding good. Got a title for it yet?"

I nod towards RJ's guitar. I've heard snatches of this tune a few times now, and bits of it are already sticking in my head.

"Nope, haven't got any lyrics – just some chords, really," RJ says with a smile and a shrug. "I'm waiting for inspiration to strike. I'm hoping it might, now we're back home."

"And it's so good to be back here, isn't it, Minnie?" Mum says to my pup in the sort of silly voice humans can't help using on dogs.

As Mum scratch-scratches at Minnie's ear, I see the white star on her wrist. I look over at RJ, and picture the matching star on his right wrist as he strums the strings.

White stars for love; love for Weezy, for Mum and for RJ.

White stars that match the name of RJ's band.

"RJ," I begin, as a question snakes its way to the forefront of my mind. "How come you called yourselves White Star Line?"

I'm remembering snippets of what Cam read out to me from the magazine article. In the shock of it all, the mention of the shipping company's name had passed me by – till now.

"Wow! Where did that question come from?" laughs RJ. "Well, when we were starting out, me and the lads shared a flat. We'd rehearse, then come home and stay up late watching whatever was on the History or Discovery channels. One night, there was this fantastic documentary on about the *Titanic* ..."

The sun is warm on my shoulders, but shivers quiver up my back.

"... and at one point, they mentioned that the shipping company that owned the *Titanic* was called White Star Line," RJ carries on, unaware of the effect his words are having on me. "I just looked around at the other guys and said, 'That's it! That's our name!' Funny how things happen out of the blue, and then feel like they're meant to be, somehow."

Like we're meant to be here, somehow, I think, looking up at the grey granite of Wilderwood Hall.

And in that second I know I am not special and never was a "seer".

Wilderwood is what's special.

Wilderwood called out to *me* the most, but to all of us in different ways, at different times, sending out its whispers, drawing us here to tell its story and stop it from rotting away in loneliness.

It tried with the hippy guy decades ago, filling his head and his dreams with visions of a sea where it shouldn't be, miles and miles and *miles* from a shore. It was too much for him.

And what *I* saw those first few days was almost too much for me to handle. But now – apart from the sometimes sad surprise of the magazine article – I feel peaceful, happy and right. And so does the house.

"Does that answer your question, Ellis?" RJ asks, smiling up at me, his eyes squinting against the sunlight.

"Uh, yeah," I say, so caught up in my own thoughts that I'm trying to remember what my stepdad just said.

"So what've you got there, babe?" asks Mum,

noticing that I've been distractedly swivelling the rolled-up magazine around in my hands like a baton.

"It's an article about the history of Wilderwood Hall," I tell Mum, handing her the magazine, since RJ's got his hands full with his guitar. "You both need to read it."

Mum lets go of Minnie to take the mag from me, and Minnie uses the opportunity to scamper off on new adventures.

I'm glad of the distraction. I'll leave Mum and RJ to read about what happened to all those long-gone people whose lives I briefly brushed up against when I slipped into their world, like a shadow from the future. . .

"Better go catch Minnie – back in a sec!" I call out to Mum and RJ as I hurry around the corner of the building in pursuit of my pup.

As soon as I'm out of sight, I slow down.

Minnie is fine, I can see, happily playing with an old pine cone she's found. So I flop down on the edge of the fountain that's out of sight of the terrace and watch her, all the while idly running one hand over the dark earth that Mum's been digging and loosening.

Breathe, I tell myself, trying to get my heart rate back to normal.

Breathe, I say again, as my fingers work down into the soft, cool soil.

Breathe. . .

Suddenly, I turn stiff and still, my burrowing hand sensing an unexpected change.

A coldness, a steely, shockingly bitter coldness. A deep, almost icy chill that's *wet*.

I stare down.

Water is lapping at my wrist.

Bending, staring, I see that the depths of it seem to have no end. It's as bottomless as some faraway ocean, light refracting and shifting and being swallowed by the deep blue.

And something's down there.

Someone.

I've been telling myself to breathe, but now take a deep, sharp gulp of air in. I'm startled – but not frightened – when I see that the someone is Flora.

She's fading away from me, sinking, sinking, arms star-shaped and eyes staring up into mine.

As she sinks further and begins to disappear into the watery shadows, I can just make out her mouth moving. I tilt forward and peer harder, trying to make out what she's trying to tell me.

"Sorry," Flora is mumbling, over and over and over again, her urgent words rising in bubbles and the whisperings of them tingling my fingertips.

Then she's gone, vanished into nothingness, and my hand is lying in the soft earth again. I stare at the brown dirt, glad of the solid feel of it after gazing into the swirling, tilting, shifting uncertainty of the water.

Breathe. . .

I don't know how many minutes pass by in this numb blur, but I'm pulled back into the moment by Minnie tugging at the laces on my trainers.

"Hey, you!" I say with a smile, and bend down to scoop her up.

Cuddling her warm, soft body to my chest, I look around at the fountain, and wonder if it would be better to keep it this way. Maybe I'll suggest to Mum that we give up the idea of making the water flow and turn the fountain into a huge and beautiful planter. We could fill it with flowers – honeysuckle and terracotta roses, maybe – and I'll remember the sweet, brown-eyed girl Flora *almost* was. . .

"What do you think?" I say, gazing up at the building.

Sunlight chooses that very moment to glint on the

glass of the upstairs windows of the servants' quarters.

I'll take that as a yes. . .

"Oi! Miss Johnstone!" I hear RJ call out to me. "Where are you? This story's amazing!"

At the sound of RJ's voice, Minnie squiggles in my arms, and I set her back down on the ground and brush the earth from my hands.

"Coming!" I call back as I make my way towards the terrace, accompanied by a yelping, yapping bundle of joy, and feeling pretty full of a sudden, startling sense of joy myself.

Because I'm done with whispers, but I'll never be done with where I've found myself.

This place, these forests, those hills, the endless, ever-changing Scottish sky. . .

If my best friend Cam asked me now for three words for his challenge, I'd shout them out loud.

"Home."

"Happy."

"Wilderwood. . ."

Down the line, there was a girl
That was lost,
The story goes.

Tale told in whispers, through the years,
Never found,
The story goes.

Did she touch the sky, feel the air,
Breathe the salt, see the land?

The dream it died, and she was sunk,
Lost and never found,
The story goes...

From "Lost But Not Found", by White Star Line

The Blitz, 1941. The world is at war and London is no longer a safe place to be. Glory has been sent to the countryside, far away from everything she knows and loves. But what she doesn't know is that her life is about to change in ways she never imagined...

Maisie doesn't believe in ghosts. But when she starts at her new school, there are rumours of a long-gone girl who wanders the halls. Could this be the pale face that Maisie spotted in the art-room window at night? A ghostly friendship mystery from a much-loved author.

Life according to...

Alice B. Lovely

no ordinary nanny

Karen McCombie

Edie Evans will do anything she can to be left alone to look after herself. But then comes along the strange, the shy, the captivating Alice B. Lovely. Suddenly life is looking weirdly sparkly...